I0665437

THE DO-IT-YOURSELF PLANET

Link Denham had spent most of his adult life trying to avoid boredom. But sometimes there can be
too much adventure for any man. One morning Link
awoke, battling a fierce hangover, to find himself
aboard a rickety old spaceship, with a strange little
man named Thistlethwaite. It seemed they were
bound for an unexplored planet to collect unexplain-
ed riches.

The last ship that had tried to land on Sord III,
their unprepossessing destination, had been warned
off at risk of destruction. And Link was about to en-
counter a strange welcome. First, there were the small
pink piglike animals, who spoke in a surprisingly
human, insultingly sarcastic manner. But the second
half of the reception committee was a good deal
more formidable.

Turn this book over for
second complete novel

MURRAY LEINSTER, whose real name is Will F. Jenkins, has been entertaining the public with his exciting fiction for several decades. Called the dean of modern science-fiction, he was writing these amazing super-science adventures back in the early twenties before there ever was such a thing as an all-fantasy magazine. His short stories, novelettes, and serial novels have appeared in most of the major American magazines, both slick and pulp, and many have been reprinted all over the world. He has made a distinguished name for himself (or rather two names) in the fields of adventure, historical, western, sea, and suspense stories.

Ace Books has still available the following Murray Leinster novels: CITY ON THE MOON (D-277), THE PIRATES OF ZAN and THE MUTANT WEAPON (D-403), THE FORGOTTEN PLANET (D-528), and THIS WORLD IS TABOO (D-525).

MURRAY LEINSTER

THE DUPLICATORS

ACE BOOKS, INC.
1120 Avenue of the Americas
New York, N.Y. 10036

I

I T OCCURRED to Link Denham, as a matter for mild regret, that he was about to wake up, and he'd had much too satisfactory a pre-slumber evening to want to do so. He lay between sleeping and awake, and he felt a splendid peacefulness, and the festive events in which he'd relaxed after six months on Glaeth ran pleasantly through his mind. He didn't want to think about Glaeth any more. He'd ventured forth for a large evening because he wanted to forget that man-killing world. Now, not fully asleep and very far from wide-awake, snatches of charming memory floated through his consciousness. There had been song, this past evening.

There had been conversation, man-talk upon matters of great interest and no importance whatever. And things had gone on to a remarkably enjoyable climax.

He did not stir, but he remembered that one of his new-found intimate friends had been threatened with ejection from the place where Link and others relaxed. There were protests, in which Link joined. Then there was conflict, in which he took part. The intended ejectee was rescued before he was heaved into the darkness outside this particular spaceport joint. There was celebration of his rescue. Then the spaceport cops arrived, which was an insult to all the warm friends who now considered that they had been celebrating together.

Link drowsily and pleasurably recalled the uproar. There were many pleasing items it was delightful to review. Some-body'd defied fate and chance and spaceport cops from a pyramid of piled-up chairs and tables. Link himself, with many loyal comrades, had charged the cops who tried to pull him down. He recalled bottles spinning in the air, spouting their contents as they flew. Spaceport cops turned fire hoses on Link's new friends, and they and he heaved chairs at spaceport cops. Some friends fought cordially on the floor and others zestfully at other places, and all the tensions and all the tautness of nerves developed on Glaeth—where the death rate was ten per cent a month among carynth-hunters—were relieved and smoothed out and totally erased. So Link now felt completely peaceful and beatifically content.

Somewhere, something mechanical clicked loudly. Some-thing else made a subdued grunting noise which was also mechanical. These sounds were reality, intruding upon the blissful tranquility Link now enjoyed.

He remembered something. His eyes did not open, but his hand fumbled at his waist. He was reassured. His stake-belt was still there, and it still contained the gritty small objects for which he'd risked his life several times a day for some months in succession. Those pinkish crystals were at once the reason and the reward for his journey to Glaeth. He'd been lucky. But he'd become intolerably tense. He'd been unable to relax when the buy-boat picked him up with other carynth-hunters, and he hadn't been able to loosen up his nerves at the planet to which the buy-boat took him. But here, on this remoter planet, Trent, he had relaxed at last. He was soothed. He was prepared to face reality with a cheerful confidence.

Remembering, he had become nearly awake. It occurred to him that the laws of the planet Trent were said to be severe. The cops were stern. It was highly probable that when he opened his eyes he would find himself in jail, with fines to be paid and a magistrate's lecture on proper behavior to be listened to. But he recalled unworriedly that he could pay his fines, and that he was ready to behave like an angel, now that he'd relaxed.

The loud clicking sound repeated. It was followed again by the grunting noise. Link opened his eyes.

Something that looked like a wall turned slowly around some six feet away from him. A moment later he found himself regarding a corner where three walls came together. He hadn't moved his head. The wall moved. Again, later, a square and more or less flat object with a billowing red cloth on it floated into view. He deduced that it was a table.

He was not standing on his feet, however. He was not lying on a bunk. He floated, weightless, in mid-air in a cubicle perhaps ten feet by fifteen and seven feet high. The thing with the red cloth on it was truly a table, fastened to what ought to be a floor. There were chairs. There was a doorway with steps leading nowhere.

Link closed his eyes and counted ten, but the look of things remained the same when he reopened them. Before his relaxation of the night before, such a waking would have disturbed him. Now he contemplated his surroundings with calm. He was evidently not in jail. As evidently, he was not aground anywhere. The only possible explanation was unlikely to the point of insanity, but it had to be true. He was in a spaceship, and not a luxurious one. This particular compartment was definitely shabby. And on the evidence of no-gravity, the ship was in free fall. It was not exactly a normal state of things to wake up to.

There came again a loud clicking, followed by another subdued mechanical grunt. Link made a guess at the origin of the sounds. It was most likely a pressure-reduction valve releasing air from a high-pressure tank to maintain a lower pressure somewhere else. If Link had taken thought, his hair would have stood on end immediately. But he didn't.

The cubicle, moving sedately around him, brought one of its walls within reach of his foot. He kicked. He floated away from the ceiling to a gentle impact on the floor. He held on, more or less, by using the palms of his hands as suction-cups—a most unsatisfactory system—and got within reach of a table-leg. He swung himself about and shoved for the doorway. He floated to it in slow motion, caught hold of a stair-tread, got a grip on the door frame, and oriented himself with respect to the room.

He was in the mess room of a certainly ancient and obviously small ship of space. All was shabbiness. Where paint had not peeled off, it stayed on in blisters. The flooring was worn through to the metal plates beneath. There were other signs of neglect. There had been no tidying of this mess room for a long time.

He heard a faint, new, rumbling sound. It stopped, and came again. It was overhead, in the direction the stairway led to. The rumbling came once more. It was rhythmic.

Link grasped a hand-rail and heaved himself gently upward. He arrived at a landing, and the rumbling noise was louder. This level of the ship contained cabins for the crew. The rumbling came from a higher level still. He went up more steps, floating as before.

He arrived at a control-room which was antiquated and grubby and of very doubtful efficiency. There were ports, which were covered with frost.

Somebody snored above his head. That was the rumbling sound. Link lifted his eyes and saw the snorer. A small, whiskery man scowled portentiously even in his sleep. He floated in mid-air as Link had floated, but with his knees drawn up and his two hands beside his cheek as if resting on an imaginary pillow. And he snored.

Link reflected, and then said genially,

"Hello!"

The whiskery man snored again. Link saw something familiar about him. Yes. He'd been involved in the festivity of the night before. Link remembered having seen him scowling ferociously from the side lines while tumult raged and firehoses played.

"Ship ahoy!" said Link loudly.

The small man jumped, in the very middle of a snore. He choked and blinked and made astonished movements, and of course began to turn eccentric half-circles in mid-air. In one of his turnings he saw Link. He said peevishly,

"Dammit, don't stand there starin'! Get me down! But don't turn on the gravity! Want me to break my neck?"

Link reached up and caught a foot. He brought the little man down to solidity and released him.

"Huh!" said the little man waspishly. "You're awake."

"Apparently," admitted Link. "Are you?"

The little man snorted. He aligned himself and gave a shove. He floated through the air to the control board. He caught its corner. He looked it over and pushed a button. Ship gravity came on. There was a sudden slight jolt, and then a series of lesser jolts, and then the fine normal feeling of gravity and weight and up and down. Things abruptly

9

looked more sensible. They weren't, but they looked that way.

"I'm curious," said Link. "Have you any idea where we are?"

The whiskery man said scornfully,

"Where we are? How'd I know? That's your business!"

His air grew truculent as Link didn't grasp the idea.

"My business?"

"You're the astrogator, ain't you? You signed on last night; I had to help you hold the pen, but you signed on! Astrogator, third officer's ticket, and you said you could astrogate a wash bucket from Sirius Three to the Rim with nothin' but a root-rule and a logarithm table. That's what you said! You said you'd astrogated a Norse spaceliner six hundred lightyears tail-first to port after her overdrive unit switched poles. You said—"

Link held up his hand.

"I . . . er . . . I recognize the imaginative style," he said painfully. "It's mine, in my more exuberant moments. But how did that land me . . . wherever I am?"

"You made a deal with me," said the little man, truculently. "Thistlethwaite's the name. You signed on this ship, the *Glamorgan*, an' you said you were an astrogator and I made the deal on that representation. It's four years in jail, on Trent, to sign on or act as a astrogator unless you're duly licensed."

"Morbid people, the lawmakers of Trent," said Link. "What else?"

"You don't draw wages," said the whiskery man, as truculently as before. "You're a junior partner in the business I'm startin'. You agreed to leave all matters þut astrogation to me, on penalty of forfeitin' all moneys due or accrued or to accrue. It's a tight contract. I wrote it myself."

"I am lost in admiration," said Link politely. "But—"

"We're goin'," said Thistlethwaite sternly, "to a planet I know. Another fella and me, we landed there in a spaceboat

10

after the ship we was in got wrecked. We made a deal with the . . . uh . . . authorities. We took off again in the spaceboat. It was loaded down with plenty valuable cargo! We was to go back, but my partner—he was the astrogator of the spaceboat—he took his share of the money and started celebratin'! Two weeks later he jumped out a window because he thought pink gryphs was coming out of the wall after him. That left me sole owner of the business, but strapped for cash. I'd been celebratin' too. So I bought the *Glamorgan* with what I had, an' bought a cargo for her."

"A very fine ship, the *Glamorgan*," said Link, politely. "But I'm a little dense this morning, or evening, or whatever it may be. How do I fit into the picture of commercial enterprise aboard this splendid ship the *Glamorgan?*"

The whiskery man spat, venomously.

"The ship's junk," he snapped. "I couldn't get papers for her to go anywheres but to a junk yard on Bellaire to be scrapped. I hadda astrogator and a fella to spell me in the engine room. They believed we was going to the junk yard, but we had some trouble with the engines layin' down, and she leaked air. Plenty! So when we got to Trent those two run off. They're liable to two years in jail for runnin' out on a contract concernin' personal services. Hell! They didn't think we'd make Trent! They wanted to take to the spaceboat and abandon ship halfway there! And me with all my capital tied up in it!"

Link regarded his companion uncomfortably. Thistlethwaite snapped,

"So I was stuck on Trent with no astrogator an' port-dues pilin' up. Until you came along."

"Ah!" said Link. "I came along! Riding a white horse, no doubt, and kissing my hand to the ladies. Then what?"

"I asked you if you was a astrogater, and you told me yes."

"I hate to disappoint people," said Link regretfully. "I probably wanted to brighten up your day, or evening. I tried."

"Then," said Thistlethwaite portentiously, "I told you enough about what I'm goin' after so you said it was a splendid venture, befittin' such men as you and me. You'd join me, you said. But you wanted to fight some more policemen before liftin' off. I'd already drug you out of a fight where the spaceport cops was usin' fire-hoses on both sides. I told you fightin' policemen carries six months in jail, on Trent. But you wouldn't listen. Even after I told you why we had to take off quick."

"And that reason was—"

"Spaceport dues," snapped the little man. "On the *Glamorgan!* Landin'-grid fees. On the *Glamorgan!* I run out of money! Besides, there was grub and some parts for the engines that'd been givin' trouble. I bought 'em and charged 'em, like a business man does, expectin' to come back some day and pay for 'em. But the spaceport people got suspicious. They were goin' to seize the ship tomorrow—today—and sell her if they could for the port bills and grub bills and parts bills."

"I see!" said Link. "And I probably sympathized with you."

"You said," said the little man grimly, "that it was a conspiracy against brave an' valiant souls like us two, an' you'd only fight two more policemen—six months more on top of what you was already liable to—and then we'd defy such crass and commercial individuals and take off into the wild blue yonder."

Link reflected. He shook his head in mild disapproval.

"So what happened?"

"You fought four policemen," said his companion succinctly. "In two separate scraps, addin' a year in jail to what you'd piled up before."

"It begins to look," said Link, "as if I may have made myself unpopular on Trent. Is there anything else I ought to know?"

"They started to use tear gas on you," the whiskery man told him, "so you set fire to a police truck. To let the flames lift up the gas, you said. That would be some more years in jail. But I got you in the *Glamorgan*—"

"And got the grid to lift us off?" When the little man shook his head, Link asked hopefully. "I got the grid to lift us off? . . . We persuaded—"

"Nope," said Thistlethwaite. "You just took off. On emergency rockets. Off the spaceport tarmac. With no clearance. Leavin' the oiled tarmac on fire." Link winced. The little man went on inexorably, "We hit for space at six gees accelleration and 'near as I can make out you kept goin' at that till the first rockets burned out. And then you went down into the mess room."

"I suppose," said Link unhappily, "that I'd worked up an appetite. Or was there some way I could pile up a few more years to spend in jail?"

"You went to sleep," said the little man. "And I wasn't goin' to bother you!"

Link thought it over.

"No," he agreed. "I can see that you mightn't have wanted to bother me. Do you intend to turn around and go back to Trent?"

"What for?" demanded the little man bitterly. "For jail? An' for them to sell off the *Glamorgan* for port dues and such?"

"There's that, of course," acknowledged Link. "But I'd rather believe you wouldn't leave a friend in distress, or jail. All right. I don't want to go back to Trent either. I'm an outdoorsy sort of character and I wouldn't like to spend the next eighteen years in jail."

"Twenty-two," said Thistlethwaite. "And six months."

"So," finished Link, "I'll play along. Since I'm the astrogator I'll try to find out where we are. Then you'll tell me where you want to go. And after that, some evening when there's nothing special to do, you'll tell me why. Right?"

"The why," snapped the whiskery man, "is I promised

13

to make you so rich y'couldn't spend the interest on y'money! And you a junior partner!"

"Carynths?" suggested Link.

Carynths were the galaxy's latest and most fabulous status gems. They couldn't be synthesized—they were said to be the result of meteoric impacts on a special peach-colored ore—and they were as beautiful as they were rare. So far they'd only been found on Glaeth. But if a woman had a carynth ring, she was somebody. If she had a carynth bracelet, she was Somebody. And if she had a carynth necklace, she ruled society on the planet on which she was pleased to reside. But—

"Carynths are garbage," said Thisthethwaite contemptuously, "alongside of what's waitin' for us! For each one of what I'm tradin' for, to bring it away from where we're goin', I'll get a hundred million credits an' half the profits after that! An' I'll have a shipload of e'm! And it's all set! Now you do your stuff and I'll check over the engines."

He headed down the stairwell. He reached the first landing below. The second. Link heard a faint click and then a mechanical grunting noise. At the sound, the little man howled enragedly. Link jumped.

"What's the matter?" he asked anxiously.

"We're leakin' air!" roared the little man. "Bleedin' it! You musta started some places, takin' off at six gees! All the air's pourin' out!"

His words became unintelligible, but they were definitely profane. Doors clanged shut, cutting off his voice. He was sealing all compartments.

Link surveyed the control room of the ship. In his younger days he'd aspired to be a spaceman. He'd been a cadet in the Merchant Space Academy on Malibu for two complete terms. Then the faculty let him go. He liked novelty and excitement and on occasion, tumult. The faculty didn't. His grades were all right but they heaved him out. So he knew

14

a certain amount about astrogation. Not much, but enough to keep from having to go back to Trent.

A door closed below. The little man's voice could be heard, swearing sulfurously. He got something from somewhere and the door clanged behind him again, cutting off his voice once more.

Link resumed his survey. There was the control board, reasonably easy to understand. There was the computer, simple enough for him to operate. There were reference books. A *Galactic Directory* for this sector. Alditch's *Practical Astrogation*. A luridly bound volume of *Space-Commerce Regulations*. The *Directory* was brand new. The others were old and tattered volumes.

Link went carefully over the ship's log, which contained every course steered, time elapsed, and therefore distance run in parsecs and fractions of them. He could take the *Glamorgan* back to the last three ports she'd visited by reversing the recorded maneuvers. But that didn't seem enterprising.

He skimmed through the *Astrogator*. He'd be somewhere not too many millions of miles from the sun of the planet *Trent*. He'd take a look at the Trent listing in the *Directory*, copy out its coordinates and proper motion, check the galactic poles and zero galactic longitude by observation out the ports, and then get at the really tricky stuff when he learned the ship's destination.

He threw on the heater switch so he could see out the ports and observe the sun which shone on Trent. Instantly an infuriated bellow came up from below.

"Turn off the heat!" raged Thistlethwaite from below. "Turn it off!"

"But the ports are frosted," Link called back. "I need to see out! We need the heaters!"

"I was sittin' on one! Turn 'em off!"

A door clanged below. Link shrugged. If Thistlethwaite

had to sit on a heater, the heater shouldn't be on. Delay was indicated.

He wasn't worried. The mood of tranquility and repose he'd waked with still stayed with him. Naturally! His current situation might have seemed disturbing to somebody else, but to a man who'd just left the planet Glaeth, with its strictly murderous fauna and flora and climatic conditions, to be aboard a merely leaking spaceship of creaking antiquity was restful. That it was only licensed to travel to a junk yard for scrapping seemed no cause for worry. That it was bound on a mysterious errand instead seemed interesting. With no cares whatever, Link was charmed to find himself in a situation where practically anything was more than likely to happen.

He thought restfully of not being on Glaeth. There were animals there which looked like rocks and acted like stones until one got within reach of remarkably extensible hooked claws. There were trees which dripped a corrosive fluid on any moving creature that disturbed them. There were gigantic flying things against which the only defense was concealment, and things which tunneled underground and made traps into which anything heavier than a rabbit would drop as the ground gave way beneath it. And there was the climate. In the area in which the best finds of carynths had been made, there was no record of rain having ever fallen, and noon temperature in the most favorable season hovered around a hundred forty in the shade. But it was the only world on which carynths were to be found. The carynth-prospectors who landed there, during the most favorable season, of course, sometimes got rich. Much more often they didn't. Only forty per cent of those set aground at the beginning of the prospecting season met the buy-boat which came for them at its close. Link had been one of that lucky minority. Naturally he did not feel alarm on the *Glamorgan*. He'd almost gotten used to Glaeth! So he waited peacefully until Thisthlethwaite said it was all right to turn on the heaters and melt the frost off the ports.

He began to set up for astrogation. The coordinates for Trent would go into the computer, and then the coordinates for the ship's destination. The computer would figure the course between them and its length in parsecs and fractions of parsecs. One would drive on that course. One could, if it was desirable, look for possible ports of call on the way. Link took down the *Directory* to set up the first figures.

He happened to notice a certain consequence of the *Directory*'s newness. It was the only un-shabby, un-worn object on the ship. But even it showed a grayish, well-thumbed line on the edge of certain pages which had been often referred to. The grayishness should be a guide to the information about Trent, as the *Glamorgan*'s latest port of call. Link opened the grayest page, pleased with himself for his acuteness.

But Trent wasn't listed on that page. Trent wasn't even in that part of the book. The heading of this particular chapter of listings was, "*Non-Cluster Planets Between Huyla and Glaire.*" It described the maverick solar systems not on regular trade-routes and requiring long voyages from commercial spaceports if anybody was to reach them. People rarely wanted to.

Link stared. He found signs that this had been repeatedly referred to by somebody with engine-oil on his fingers. One page had plainly been read and re-read and re-read. The margin was darkened as if an oily thumb had held a place there while the item was gloated over.

From any normal standpoint it was not easy to understand.

"SORD" said the *Directory*. There followed the galactic coordinates to three places of decimals. "*Yel. sol-type approx. 1.4 sols mass, mny faculae all times, spectrum—*"

The spectrum-symbols could be skipped. If one wanted to be sure that a particular sun was such-and-such, one would

17

take a spectrophoto and compare it with the *Directory*. Otherwise the spectrum was for the birds. Link labored over the abbreviations that compilers of reference books use to make things difficult.

"*3rd. pl. blved. hab. ox atm. 2/3 sea nml brine, usual icecaps cloud-systems hab. est. 1.*"

Then came the interesting part. In the clear language that informative books use with such reluctance, he read:

"This planet is said to have been colonized from Surheil 11 some centuries since, and may be inhabited but no spaceport is known to exist. The last report on this planet was from a spaceyacht some two centuries ago. The yacht called down asking permission to land and was threatened with destruction if it did. The yacht took pictures from space showing specks that could be villages or the ruins of same, but this is doubtful. No other landings or communications are known. Any records which might have existed on Suheil 11 were destroyed in the Economic Wars on that planet."

In the *Glamorgan's* control room, Link was intrigued. He went back to the abbreviations and deciphered them. Sord was a yellow sol-type sun with a mass of 1.4 sols and many faculae. Its third planet was believed habitable. It had an oxygen atmosphere, two-thirds of its surface was sea, the sea was normal brine and there were the usual ice caps and cloud systems of a planet whose habitability was estimated at one.

And two centuries ago its inhabitants had threatened to smash a spaceyacht which wanted to land on it.

According to Thistlethwaite, the bill for last evening's relaxation, for Link, amounted to twenty-some years to be served in jail. Even with some sentences running concurrently, it was preferable not to return to Trent. On the other hand—

THE DUPLICATORS

But it didn't really need to be thought about. Thistle-thwaite plainly intended to go to Sord Three, whose inhabitants strongly preferred to be left alone. But they seemed to have made an exception in his favor. He was so anxious to get there and so confident of a welcome that he'd bought the *Glamorgan* and loaded her up with freight, and he'd taken an unholy chance in his choice of a ship. He'd taken another in depending on Link as an astrogator. But it would be a pity to disappoint him!

So Link carefully copied down in the log the three co-ordinates of Sord Three, and hunted up its proper solar motion, and put that in the log, and then put the figures for Trent in the computer and copied the answer in the log, too. It seemed the professional thing to do. Then he scraped away frost from the ports and got observations of the *Glamorgan's* current heading, and went back to the board and adjusted that. He was just entering the last item in the log when Thistlethwaite came in. His hands were black from the work he'd done, and somehow he gave the impression of a man who had used up all his store of naughty words and still was unrelieved.

"Well?" asked Link pleasantly.

"We're leakin' air," said the whiskered man bitterly. "It's whistlin' out! Playin' tunes as it goes! I had to seal off the spaceboat blister. If we need that spaceboat we'll be in a fix! When my business gets goin', I'll never use another junk ship like this! You raised hell in that take-off!"

"It's very bad?" asked Link.

"I shut off all the compartments I couldn't seal tight," said Thistlethwaite bitterly. "And there's still some leakage in the engine room, but I can't find it. I ain't found it so far, anyways!"

Link said,

"How's the air supply?"

"I pumped up on Trent," said the little man. "If they'd known, they'd ha' charged me for that, too!"

"Can we make out for two weeks?" asked Link.

"We can make out for ten!" snapped the whiskery one. "There's only two of us an' we can seal off everything but the control room an' the engine room an' a way between 'em. We can go ten weeks!"

"Then," said Link relievedly, "we're all right." He made final adjustments. "The engines are all right?"

He looked up pleasantly, his hand on a switch.

"With coddlin'," said Thistlethwaite. "What're you doin'?" he demanded suspiciously. "I ain't give you—"

Link threw the circuit-completing switch. The universe seemed to reel. Everything appeared to turn inside out, including Link's stomach. He had the feeling of panicky fall in a contracting spiral. The lights in the control room dimmed almost to extinction. The whiskery man uttered a strangled howl. This was the normal experience when going into overdrive travel at a number of times the speed of light.

Then, abruptly, everything was all right again. The vision-ports were dark, but the lights came back to full brightness. The *Glamorgan* was in overdrive, hurtling through emptiness very, very much faster than theory permitted in the normal universe. But the universe immediately around the *Glamorgan* was not normal. The ship was in an overdrive field, which does not occur normally, at all.

"What the hell've you done?" raged Thistlethwaite. "Where you headed for? I didn't tell you—"

"I'm driving the ship," said Link pleasantly, "for a place called Sord Three. There ought to be some good business prospects there. Isn't that where you want to go?"

The little man's face turned purple. He glared.

"How'd you find that out?" he demanded ferociously.

"Why, I've got friends there," said Link untruthfully.

The little man leaped for him, uttering howls of fury.

THE DUPLICATORS

Link turned off the ship's gravity. Thistlethwaite wound up bouncing against the ceiling. He clung there, swearing. Link kept his hand on the gravity button. At any instant he could throw the gravity back on, and as immediately off again.

"Tut, tut!" said Link reproachfully. "Such naughty words. And I thought you'd be pleased to find your junior partner displaying energy and enthusiasm and using his brains loyally to further the magnificent business enterprise we've started!"

II

THE *Glamorgan* bored on through space. Not normal space, of course. In the ordinary sort of space between suns and planets and solar systems generally, a ship is strictly limited to ninety-eight-point-something per cent of the speed of light, because mass increases with speed, and inertia increases with mass. But in an overdrive field the properties of space are modified. The effect of a magnet on iron is changed past recognition. The effect of electrostatic stress upon dielectrics is wholly abnormal. And inertia, instead of multiplying itself with high velocity, becomes as undetectable as at zero velocity. In fact, theory says that a ship has no velocity on an overdrive field. The speed is of the field itself. The ship is carried. It goes along for the ride.

But there was no thinking about such abstractions on the *Glamorgan*. The effect of overdrive was the same as if the ship did pierce space at many times the speed of light. Obviously, light from ahead was transposed a great many octaves upward, into something as different from light as long-wave radiation is from heat. This radiation was refracted outward from the ship by the overdrive field, and was therefore without effect upon instruments or persons. Light from behind was left there. Light from the sides was also refracted outward and away. The *Glamorgan* floated at ease in a hurtling, unsubstantial space-stress center, and to try to understand it might produce a headache, but hardly anything more useful.

But though the *Glamorgan* in overdrive attained the end of speed without the need for velocity, the human relationship between Link and Thistlethwaite was less simple. The whiskery little man was impassioned about his enterprise. Link had guessed his highly secret destination, and Thistlethwaite was outraged by the achievement. Even when Link showed him how Sord Three had been revealed as the objective of the voyage, Thistlethwaite wasn't mollified. He clamped his lips shut tightly. He refused to give any further intimation about what he proposed to do when he arrived at Sord Three. Link knew only that he'd touched ground there in a space-boat with one companion and they'd left with a valuable cargo, and now Thistlethwaite was bound back there again, if Link could get him there.

There were times when it seemed doubtful. Then Link blamed himself for trying it. Still, Thistlethwaite had chosen the *Glamorgan* on his own and had gotten as far as Trent in her. But there were times when it didn't appear that the ship would ever get anywhere else. The log book had a plenitude of emergencies written in its pages as the *Glamorgan* went onward.

She leaked air. They didn't try to keep the inside pressure up to the standard 14.7 pounds. They compromised on eleven, because they'd loose less air at the lower pressure. Even so, the fact that the *Glamorgan* leaked was only one of her oddities. She also smelled. Her air system was patched and

her generators were cobbled, and at odd moments she made
unrefined noises for no reason that anybody could find out.
The water pressure system sometimes worked and sometimes
did not. The refrigeration unit occasionally turned on when
it shouldn't and sometimes didn't when it should. It was
wise to tap the thermostat several times a day to keep
frozen stores from thawing.

The overdrive field generator was also a subject for nightmares. Link didn't understand overdrive, but he did know
that a field shouldn't be kept in existence by hand-wound
outer layers on some of the coils, with wedges driven in
to keep contacts tight which ought to be free to cut off
in case of emergency. But it could be said that everything
about the ship was an emergency. Link would have come
to have a very great respect for Thistlethwaite because he
kept such tinkered wreckage working. But he was appalled
at the idea of anybody deliberately trusting his life to it.

The thing was, he realized ultimately, that Thistlethwaite
was an eccentric. The galaxy is full of crackpots, each of
whom has mysterious secret information about illimitable
wealth to be found on the non-existent outer planets of
rarely visited suns, or in the depths of the watery satellites
of Cepheids. But crackpots only talk. Their ambition is to
be admired as men of mystery and vast secret knowledge.
They will never try actually to find the treasures they claim
to know about. If you offer to provide a ship and crew to
pick up the riches they describe in such detail, they'll im-
pose impossible conditions. They don't want to risk their
dreams by trying to make them come true.

But Thistlethwaite wasn't that way. He wasn't a crackpot.
In his description of the wealth awaiting him, Link considered that he must be off the beam. There was no such
treasure in the galaxy. But he'd been on Sord Three, and
he'd had some money—enough to buy the *Glamorgan* and
her cargo—and he was trying to get back. He'd cut Link

in out of necessity, because the *Glamorgan* had to get off Trent when she did, or not get off at all. So Thistlethwaite was not a crackpot. But an eccentric, that he was!

Fuming but resolute, the little man tried valiantly to make the ship hold together until his project was completed. From the beginning four compartments besides the spaceboat blister were sealed off because they couldn't be made airtight. A fifth compartment lost half a pound of air every hour on the hour. Thistlethwaite labored over it, daubing extinguisher-foam on joints and cracks until he found where the foam vanished first. Then he lavishly applied sealing-compound. This was not the act of a crackpot who only wants to be admired. It was consistent with a far-out mentality which would run the wildest of risks to carry out a purpose. Moreover, when after days of labor he still couldn't bring the air loss down below half a pound a day, he sealed off that compartment too. The *Glamorgan* had been a tub to begin with. Now she displayed characteristics to make a reasonably patient man break down and cry.

Link offered to help in the sealing-off process. Thistlethwaite snapped at him.

"You tend to your knitting and I'll tend to mine," he said acidly. "You're so smart at workin' out things I want to keep to myself."

"I only found out where we're going," said Link. "I didn't find out why."

"To get rich," snapped Thistlethwaite. "That's why! I want to get rich! I spent my life bein' poor. Now I want to get kowtowed to! My first partner got money and he couldn't wait to enjoy it. I've waited. I'm not telling anybody anything! I know what I'm goin' to do. I got a talent for business. I never had a chance to use it. No capital. Now I'm going to get rich and do things like I always wanted to do."

Link asked more questions and the little man turned waspishly upon him.

"That's my business, like runnin' this ship to where we're goin' is yours! You leave me be! I'm not riskin' you knowin' what I know. I'm not takin' the chance of you figurin' you'll do better cheating me than playin' fair."

This was shrewdness, after a fashion. There are plenty of men who quite simply and naturally believe that the way to profit in any enterprise is to double-cross their associates. The whiskery man had evidently met them. He wasn't sure Link wasn't one of them. He kept his mouth shut.

"Eventually," said Link, "I'm going to have to come out of overdrive to check my course. Is that all right with you?"

"That's your business!" rasped Thistlethwaite. "You tend to your business and I'll tend to mine!"

He disappeared, prowling around the ship, checking the air pressure, spending long periods in the engine room and not unfrequently coming silently and secretly up the stairway to the control room to regard Link with inveterate suspicion.

It annoyed Link. So when he determined that he should break out of overdrive to verify his position—a dubious business considering the limits of his knowledge—he did not notify Thistlethwaite. He simply broke out of overdrive.

There should have been merely an instant of intolerable vertigo and of intense nausea, and then the sensation of a spiral fall toward infinity, but nothing more. Those sensations occurred. But as they began there was also a wild, rasping roar in the engine room. Lights dimmed. Thistlethwaite howled with fury and flung himself down into an inferno of blue arcs and stinking scorched insulation. In that incredible nightmare-like atmosphere he hit something with a stick. He pulled violently on a rope. He spun a wheel rapidly. And the arcs died. The ship's ancient air system began to struggle with the smoke and smells.

It took him two days to make repairs, during which he did

not address one syllable to Link. But Link was busy anyhow. He was taking observations and checking the process with the *Practical Astrogator* as he went along. Then he used the computer to make his observations mean something. He faithfully wrote all these exercises in the ship's log. It helped to pass the time. But when determination of the ship's position by three different methods gave the same result, he arrived at the astonishing conclusion that the *Glamorgan* was actually on course.

He was composing a tribute to himself for the feat when Thistlethwaite came bristling into the control room.

"I fixed what you messed up," he said bitterly. "We can go on now. But next time you do something, don't do it till you ask me, and I'll fix it so you can. You could've wrecked us."

Link opened his mouth to ask what could be a more complete wreck than the *Glamorgan* right now, but he refrained. He arranged for Thistlethwaite to go down into the engine room. He shouted down the stairways. Thistlethwaite bellowed a reply. Link checked the ship's heading again, glanced at the ship's chronometer, and threw the overdrive on.

Nothing happened except vertigo and nausea and the feeling of falling in a spiral fashion toward nowhere at all. The *Glamorgan* was again in overdrive. The little man came in, brushing off his hands.

"That's the way," he said truculently, "to handle this ship!"

Link scribbled a memo of the instant the *Glamorgan* had gone into overdrive.

"In two days, four hours, thirty-three minutes and twenty seconds," he observed, "we'll want to break out again. We ought to be somewhere near Sord, then."

"If," said Thistlethwaite suspiciously, "*if* you're not tryin' to put something over on me!"

Link shrugged. He'd begun to wonder, lately, why he'd

come on this highly mysterious journey. In one sense he'd had good reason. Jail. But now he began to be restless. He wore a stake-belt next to his skin, and in it he had certain small crystals. There were people who would murder him enthusiastically for those crystals. There were others who would pay him very large sums for them. The trouble was that he had no specific idea of what he wanted to do with a large sum. Small sums, yes. He could relax with them. But large ones— He felt a need for the pleasingly unexpected. Even the exciting.

One day passed and he was definitely impatient. He was bored. He couldn't even think of anything to write in the log book. There'd been a girl about whom he'd felt romantic, not so long ago. He tried to think sentimentally about her. He failed. He hadn't seen her in months and she was probably married to somebody else now. The thought didn't bother him. It was annoying that it didn't. He craved excitement and interesting happenings, and he was merely heading for a planet that hadn't made authenticated contact with the rest of the galaxy in two hundred years, and then had promised to shoot anybody who landed. He was only in a leaky ship whose machinery broke down frequently and might at any time burn out.

He was, in a word, bored.

The second day passed. Four hours, thirty-three minutes remained. He tried to hope for interesting events. He knew of no reason to anticipate them. If Thistlethwaite were right, there would be only business dealings aground, and presently an attempt to get to somewhere else in the *Glamorgan*, and after that—

The whiskery man went down into the engine room and bellowed that everything was set. Link sat by the control board, leaning on his elbows, in a mood of deep skepticism. He didn't believe anything in particular was likely to happen. Especially he didn't believe in Thistlethwaite's story of fabulous wealth. There was nothing as valuable as Thistle-thwaite described. Such things simply didn't exist. But since he'd come this far—

Two minutes to go. One minute twenty seconds. Twenty seconds. Ten . . . five . . . four . . . three . . . two . . . one!

He flipped the overdrive switch to off. There were the customary sensations of dizzy fall and vertigo and nausea. Then the *Glamorgan* floated in normal space, and there was a sun not unreasonably far away, and all the sky was stars. Link was even pessimistic about the identity of the sun, but a spectro-photo identified it. It was truly Sord. There were planets. One. Two. Three. Three had ice-caps; it looked as if two-thirds of its surface was sea, and in general it matched the *Directory's* description. It might . . . just possibly . . . be inhabited.

A tediously long time later the *Glamorgan* floated in orbit around the third planet out from its sun. Mottled land masses whipped by below. There were seas, and more land masses.

Thistlethwaite watched in silence. There could be no com-munication with the ground, even if the ground was prepared to communicate. The *Glamorgan's* communication-system didn't work. Link waited for the little man to identify his destination. When it was named there would probably be trouble.

"No maps," said Thistlethwaite bitterly, on the second time around. "I asked Old Man Addison for a map but he hardly knew what I meant. They never bothered to make 'em! But Old Man Addison's Household is near a sea. Near a bay, with mountains not too far off."

Link was not relieved. It isn't easy to find a landmark of limited size on a large world from a ship in space that has no maps or even a working communicator. But on the fourth orbital circuit, clouds that had formerly hidden a certain place had moved away. Thistlethwaite pointed.

"That's it!" he said, scowling as if to cover his own doubts. "That's it! Get her down yonder!"

Link took a deep breath. Standard spaceport procedure is for a ship to call down by communicator, have coordinates supplied from the ground, get into position, and wait. Then the landing grid reaches out its forcefields and lets the ship down. It is neat, and comfortable, and safe. But there was no landing grid here. There was no information. And Link had no experience, either.

He made one extra orbit to fix the indicated landing point in his mind and to try to guess at the relative speed of ship and planetary surface. On the seventh circling of the planet, he swung the ship so it traveled stern-first and its emergency rockets could be used as retros. The drive-engine would be useless here. Thistlethwaite stayed in the control room to watch. He chewed agitatedly on wisps of whisker.

The ship hit atmosphere. There was a keening, howling sound, as if the ancient hull were protesting its own destruction. There were thumpings and bumpings. Loose plates rattled at their rivets and remaining welds.

Something came free and battered thunderously at other hull-plates before it went crazily off to nowhere. Vibration began. It became a thoroughly ominous quivering of all the ship. Link threw over the rocket lever, and the vibration ceased to increase as the emergencies bellowed below. He gave them more power, and more, until the decelleration made it difficult to stand. Then, at very long last, the vibration seemed to lessen a very little.

The ship descended into a hurricane of wind from its own motion. Unbelievable noises sounded here and there. The hole where a plate had torn away developed an organ tone with the volume of a baby earthquake's roar.

The ship hurtled on. Far ahead there was blue sea. Nearer,

there were mountains. There was a sandy look to the surface of the soil. Clouds enveloped the ship, and she came out below them, bellowing, and Link gave the rockets more braking power. But the ground still seemed to race past at an intolerable speed. He tilted the ship until her rockets did not support her at all, but only served as brakes.

Then she really went down, wallowing. He fought her, learning how to land by doing it, but without even a close idea of what it should feel like. Twice he attempted to check his descent at the cost of not checking motion toward the now-not-so-distant shoreline. He began to hope. He concentrated on matching speed with the flowing landscape.

He made it. The ship moved almost imperceptibly with respect to such landmarks as he could see. Something vaguely resembling a village appeared, far below, but he could not attend to it. The ship suddenly hovered, no more than five thousand feet high. Then Link, sweating, started to ease down.

Thistlethwaite protested agitatedly,

"I saw a village! Get her down! Get her down!"

Link cut the rockets entirely; the ship began to drop like a stone, and he cut them in again and out and in.

The *Glamorgan* landed with a tremendous crash. It teetered back and forth, making loud grinding noises. It steadied. It stopped.

Link mopped his forehead. Thistlethwaite said accusingly,

"But this ain't where we shoulda landed! We shoulda stopped by that village! And even that ain't the one I want!"

"This is where we did land," said Link, "and lucky we made it! You don't know how lucky!"

He went to a port to look out. The ship had landed in a sort of hollow, liberally sprinkled with boulders of various shapes and sizes. Sandy hillocks with sparse vegetation on their slopes appeared on every hand. Despite the ship's up-

right position, Link could not see over the hills to a true horizon.

"I'll go over to that village we saw comin' down," said
Thistlethwaite importantly, "an' arrange to send a message
to my friends. Then we'll get down to business. And there's
never been a business like this one before in all the time
since us men stopped swappin' arrowheads! You stay here an'
keep ship."

He swung the ship's one weapon, a stun gun, over his
shoulder. It gave him a rakish air. He put on a hat.

"Yep. You keep ship till I come back!"

He went down the stairs. Link heard him go down all the
levels until he came to the exit port in one of the ship's
landing fins. From the control room he saw Thistlethwaite
stride grandly to the top of the nearest hill, look ex-
haustively from there, and then march away with an air of
great and confident composure. He went out of sight beyond
the hillcrest.

Link went down to the exit port himself. The air in the
opening was fresh and markedly pleasant to breathe. He
felt that it was about time that something interesting happened. This wasn't it. Here was only commonplace landscape, commonplace sky, and commonplace tedium. He sat
on the sill of the open exit port and waited without ex-
pectation for something interesting to happen.

Presently he heard tiny clickings. Two small animals, very
much like pigs in size and appearance, came trotting hur-
riedly into view. Their hoofs had made the clicking sounds.
They saw the ship and stopped short, staring at it. They
didn't look dangerous.

"Hi, there," said Link companionably.

The small creatures vanished instantly. They plunged
behind boulders. Link shrugged. He gazed about him. After
a little, he saw an eye peering at him around a boulder. It

was the eye of one of the pig-like animals. Link moved abruptly and the eye vanished.

A voice spoke, apparently from nowhere. It was scornful. "Jumpy, huh? Scared?"

"I was startled," said Link mildly, "but I wouldn't say I was scared. Should I be?"

The voice said sardonically,

"Huh!"

There was silence again. There was stillness. A very sparse vegetation appeared to have existed where the *Glamorgan* came down on her rockets. Those scattered bits of growing stuff had been burned to ash by the rocket flames, but at the edge of the burned area some few small smouldering fragments sent threads of smoke skyward to be dissipated by wind that came over the hilltops. On a hillcrest itself a tiny sand-devil whirled for a moment and then vanished.

The voice said abruptly and scornfully,

"You in the door there! Where'd you come from?"

Link said agreeably,

"From Trent."

"What's that?" demanded the voice, disparagingly.

"A planet—a world like this," explained Link.

The voice said,

"Huh!" There was a long pause. It said, "Why?"

Link had no idea what or who his unseen questioner might be, but the tone of the questioning was scornful. He felt that a certain impressiveness on his own part was in order. He said,

"That is something to be disclosed only to proper authority. The purpose of my companion and myself, however, is entirely admirable. I may say that in time to come it is probable that the anniversary of our landing will be celebrated over the entire planet."

Having made the statement, he rather admired it. Almost anything could be deduced from it, yet it did not mean a thing.

There was again a silence. Then the voice said cagily,

"Celebrated by uffts?"

Here Link made a slight but natural error. The word "uffts," which was unfamiliar, sounded very much like "us," and he took it for the latter. He said profoundly,

"I would say that that is a reasonable assumption."

Dead silence once more. It lasted for a long time. Then the same voice said sharply,

"Somebody's coming."

There came a scurrying behind the boulders. Little clickings sounded. There were flashes of pinkish-white hide. Then the two pig-like creatures darted back into view, galloping madly for the hillcrest over which they'd come. They vanished beyond it. Link spoke again, but there was no reply.

For a long time silence lay over the hollow in which the *Glamorgan* had come to rest. Link spoke repeatedly—chattily, seriously. The silence seemed almost ominous. He began to realize that Thistlethwaite had been gone for a long time. It was well over an hour, now. He ought to be getting back.

He didn't come. Link was genuinely concerned when, at least another half-hour later, a remarkably improbable cavalcade came leisurely over the hillcrest, crossed by Thistlethwaite to begin with, and the pig-like animals later. The members of the cavalcade regarded the ship interestedly, and came on at a deliberate and unhurried pace. There were half a dozen men, mounted on large, splay-footed animals which had to be called unicorns because from the middle of their foreheads drooped flexible, flabby, horn-shaped appendages. The appendages looked discouraged. The facial expression of the animals who wore them was of complete, inquiring idiocy.

That was the first impression. The second was less pleasing. The leader of the riders wore Thistlethwaite's hat—it was too small for him—and had Thistlethwaite's stun gun slung over his shoulder. Another rider wore Thistlethwaite's shirt and a third wore the whiskery man's pants. A fourth had his shoes dangling as an ornament from his saddle. But of Thistlethwaite himself there was no sign.

All the newcomers carried long spears, lances, and wore at their belts large knives in decorated scabbards half the length of a sword.

The cavalcade came comfortably but ominously toward the *Glamorgan*. It came to a halt, its members regarding Link with expressions whose exact meaning it was not easy to decide. But Thistlethwaite had marched away from the ship with the only weapon on board, a stun rifle. The leader of this group carried it, but without any sign of familiarity with it. Link considered that he could probably get inside the ship with the port door closed before anything drastic could happen to him. He should, too, find out what had happened to Thistlethwaite. So he said,

"How do you do? Nice weather, isn't it?"

III

THERE WAS a movement among the members of the cavalcade. The leader, wearing Thistlethwaite's hat and carrying his stun rifle, looked significantly at his followers. Then he turned to Link and spoke with a certain painful politeness. There was no irony in it. It was manners. It was the most courteous of greetings.

"I'm pretty good, thank you, suh. And the weather's pretty good too, only we could do with a mite of rain." He paused, and said with an elaborate stateliness, "I'm the Householder of the Household over yonder. We heard your ship come down and we wondered about it. An' then . . . uh . . . somethin' happened and we come to look it over. We never seen a ship like this before, only o'course there's the tales from old times about 'em."

His manner was one of vast dignity. He wore Thistlethwaite's hat, and his companions or followers wore everything else that Thistlethwaite had had on in the *Glamorgan.* But he ignored the fact. It appeared that he obeyed strict rules of etiquette. And of course, people who follow etiquette are bound by it even in the preliminaries to homicide. Which is important if violence is in the air. Link took advantage of the known fact.

"It's not much of a ship," he said deprecatingly, "but such as it is I'm glad to have you see it."

The leader of the cavalcade was visibly pleased. He frowned, but he said with the same elaborate courtesy,

"My name's Harl, suh. Would you care to give me a name to call you by? I wouldn't presume for more than that."

Out of the corner of his eye Link saw that two pig-like animals had appeared not far away. They might be the same two he'd seen before. They squatted on their haunches and watched curiously what went on as between men. He said,

"My name's Link. Link Denham, in fact. Pleased to meet you."

"The same, suh! The same!" The leader's tone became warm while remaining stately. "I take that very kindly, Link, tellin' me your last name, too. And right off! Denham . . . Denham . . . I never met none of your Household before, but I'll remember it's a mannerly group. Would you . . . uh . . . have anything else to say?"

Link thought it over.

35

"I've come a long way," he observed. "I'm not sure what to say that would be most welcome."

"Welcome!" said the man who called himself Harl. He beamed. "Now, that's right nice! Boys, we been welcomed by this here Link and he's told us his last name and that's manners! This here gentleman ain't like that other fella! We're guestin'."

He slipped from his saddle, hung Thistlethwaite's stun gun on his saddle horn, and leaned his spear against the *Glamorgan*. He held out his hand cordially to Link. Link shook it. Harl's followers similarly divested themselves of weapons. They solemnly shook hands with Link. Harl rapped on one of the *Glamorgan*'s hull-plates and said admiringly,

"This here ship's iron, ain't it? M-m-m-h! I never saw so much iron to one place in all my lifetime!"

A scornful voice from somewhere said indignantly,

"We saw it first! It's ours!"

"Shut up," said Harl to the landscape at large. "And stay shut up." He turned. "Now, Link—"

"We saw it first!" insisted the voice furiously. "We saw it first! It's ours!"

"This gentleman," said Harl firmly, and again to the landscape, "is maybe thinkin' of settin' up a Household here! You uffts clear out!"

Two voices, now, insisted stridently,

"It's ours! We saw it first! It's ours!"

Harl said apologetically,

"I'm real sorry, Link, but you know how it is with uffts! Uh . . . I'd like to ask you something private."

"Come inside," said Link. He rose.

Harl and his companions—Link thought of the word "retainers" for no special reason—came trooping into the port. Link was very alertly interested. He didn't understand this state of things at all, but men with inhospitable intentions do not disarm themselves. These men had. Men with unpleasant purposes tend to cast furtive glances from one to another. These men didn't. If one ignored the presence of Thistlethwaite's garments, and the absence of Thistlethwaite himself, the atmosphere was almost insanely cordial and friendly and uncalculating. It verified past question that this planet had very little contact with other worlds. People of brisk and progressive cultures feel a deep suspicion of strangers and of each other. With reason. Yet Thistlethwaite—

Link let the small group precede him up the steps inside the landing fin. He could get down and outside before any of them, and very probably lock them in. Then he'd be armed and mounted, which in case of unfriendliness might be an advantage. But in spite of whatever had happened to Thistlethwaite, the feel of things was in no sense ominous. The visitors to the ship were openly curious and openly astonished at what they saw.

They commented almost incredulously that the long flight of steps was made of iron. Link tactfully did not refer to the sealed-off cargo compartments—the lifeboat was sealed off, too—nor to Thistlethwaite's garments worn so matter-of-factly by his guests. They passed the engine room without recognizing the door to it as what it was. They marvelled to each other that iron showed through the worn floor-covering of the mess room. They were astounded by the cabins. But the control room left them entirely uninterested except for small metal objects—instruments—fastened to the control board and fitted into the walls.

The man wearing Thistlethwaite's pants took a deep breath. He caught Link's eye and said wistfully,

"Mistuh Link, that's a right pretty little thing!"

He pointed to the ship's chronometer. Harl said angrily:

"You shut up! What kinda guest-gift have *you* brought? I beg y'pardon, Link, for this fella!" He glared at his following. "Sput! You fellas go downstairs an' wait outside,

37

so's you won't shame me again! I got to talk confidential to Mistuh Link, anyway."

His followers, still flaunting Thistlethwaite's garments, went trooping down and out. Silence fell, below. Then Harl said,

"Link, I'm right sorry about that fella! Admirin' something of yours to get it, without givin' you a gift first! I'd ought to chase him outa my Household for bad manners! I hope you'll excuse me for him!"

"No harm done," said Link. "He just forgot." It was evident that etiquette played a great part in the lives of the people of Sord Three. It looked promising. "I'd like to ask—"

Harl said confidentially,

"Let's talk private, Link. Do you know a little fella with whiskers that cusses dreadful an' insults people right an' left an' says—" his voice dropped to a shocked tone— "an' says he's a friend of Old Man Addison? A fella like that come to my Household and—you maybe won't believe this, Link, but it's so—he offered to pay me for sendin' a message to Old Man Addison! He . . . offered to . . . pay me! Like I was a ufft! I'm beggin' your pardon for askin' such a thing, but we're talkin' private. Do you know a fella like that?"

"He ran the engines of this ship," said Link. "His name's Thistlethwaite. I don't know what he has to do with Old Man Addison."

"Natural!" said Harl hastily. "I wouldn't suspect you of anything like that! But . . . uh . . . the womenfolks said his clothes wasn't duplied. Is that a fact, Link? They went crazy fingerin' the cloth he was wearin'. Was it unduplied, Link?"

"I wouldn't know anything about his clothes," said Link. "I did notice your men were wearing them. I wondered."

"But you didn't say a word," said Harl, warmly. "Yes, suh! You got manners! But did you ever hear anything like what

I just told you? Offerin' to pay me—and me a Householder—for sendin' a message to Old Man Addison! Did
you ever, Link?"

"It's bad?" asked Link, blinking.

"I left word," said Harl indignantly, "to hang him as soon
as enough folks got together to enjoy it. What else could I do?
But I'd heard the noise when this ship came down, and it
was you, landin' here! It's a great thing havin' you land
here, Link! And think of havin' clothes that ain't duplied!
If you set up a Household—"

Link stared. He'd always believed that he craved the new
and the unpredictable. But this talk left him away behind.
He felt that it would be a good idea to go off by himself
and hold his head for a while. Yet Thistlethwaite—

"Sput!" said Harl, frowning to himself. "Here I am, guestin'
with you, an' no guest-gift! But in a way you're guestin' with
me, being this is on my Household land. And I ain't been
hospitable! Look, Link! I'll send a ufft over with a message
to hold up the hangin' till we get there and we'll go watch
with the rest. What say?"

For perhaps the first time in his life, Link felt that things
were a good deal more unexpected than he entirely enjoyed.
There was only one way to stay ahead of developments until
he could sort things out.

"That suggestion," he said profoundly, "is highly consistent
with the emergency measures I feel should be substituted for
apparently standard operational procedures with reference to
discourteous space-travelers." He saw that Harl looked at
once blank and admiring, which was what he'd hoped. "In
other words," said Link, "yes."

"Then let's get started," said Harl in a pleased tone.
"Y'know, Link, you not only got manners, you got words! I
got to introduce you to my sister!"

He descended the stairs, Link following. The situation was
probably serious. It could be appalling. But Link had been

restless for days, now, from a lack of things to interest his normally active brain. He felt himself challenged. It appeared that Sord Three might turn out to be a very interesting place.

When they reached the open air, the two pig-like animals had joined the party of waiting unicorns and men. They moved about underfoot with the accustomed air of dogs with a hunting party of men. But they did not wear dogs' amiable expressions. They looked distinctly peevish.

"I want somebody to take a message," said Harl briskly. "It's worth two beers."

A pig-like animal looked at him scornfully. Link heard a voice remarkably resembling that of the invisible conversationalist he'd talked to before these men arrived.

"This is our ship!" said the voice stridently. "We saw it first!"

"You didn't tell us," said Harl firmly. "And we found it without you. Besides, it belongs to this gentleman. You want two beers?"

"Tyrant!" snapped the voice. "Robber! Grinding down the poor! Robbing—"

"Hush up!" said Harl. "Do you take the message or not?"

A second voice said defiantly,

"For four beers! It's worth ten!"

"All right, four beers it is," agreed Harl. "The message is not to hang that whiskery fella till we get there. We'll be right along."

The first scornful voice snapped,

"Who gets the message?"

"Tell my sister," said Harl impatiently. "Shoo!"

The two pig-like animals broke into a gallop together and went streaking over the nearest hill crest. As they went, squabbling voices accused each other, the one because the bargain was for only two beers apiece, and the other for having gotten himself included in the bargain out of all reason. Link stared after them, his jaw dropped open. The voices dwindled, disputing, and ended as the piggish creatures disappeared.

Link swallowed and blinked. Harl appointed one of his followers to remain in the *Glamorgan* as caretaker. That left a splay-footed animal with a drooping nose-horn as a mount for Link. Bemused and almost incredulous, he climbed into the saddle on a signal from Harl. The completely improbable cavalcade moved briskly away from the landed spaceship. It was not an indiscretion on Link's part. A caretaker remained with the ship, and Thistlethwaite was in trouble. Link went to try to get him out. Also, it appeared to be definite that Link had somehow made himself a guest in Harl's Household—whatever that might be—and etiquette protected him from ordinary peril so long as he did nothing equivalent to offering to pay to have a message delivered, or rather, so long as he did nothing equivalent to offering to pay *Harl* for having a message delivered. It was approvable to offer to pay small animals like pigs who—

"My fella back there," said Harl reassuringly as they mounted a hillock and from its top saw other hillocks stretching away indefinitely, "my fella, he'll take good care of your ship, Link. I warned him not to touch a thing but just keep uffts out and if any human come by to say you're guestin' with me."

"Thanks," said Link. Then he said painfully, "Those small fat animals—"

"Uffts?" said Harl. "Don't you have 'em where you come from?"

"No," said Link. "We don't. It seems that . . . they talk!"

"Natural," Harl agreed. "They talk too much, if you ask me. Those two will stop on the way an' tell all the other uffts all about the message, and about you, an' everything. But they were on this world when the old-timers came an' settled here. They were the smartest critters on the planet.

Plenty smart! But they're awful proud. They got brains, but they've got hoofs instead of hands, so all they can do is talk. They have big gatherin's and drink beer and make speeches to each other about how superior they are to human bein's because they ain't got paws like us."

The motion of the splay-footed unicorns was unpleasant. The one Link rode put down each foot separately, and the result was a series of swayings in various directions which had a tendency to make a rider sea-sick. Link struggled with that sensation. Harl appeared to be thinking deeply, and sadly. The unicorns were not hoofed animals so there was no sound of hoofbeats. There was only the creaking of saddle leather and very occasionally the clatter of a spear or some other object against something else.

"Y'know," said Harl presently, "I'd like to believe that you comin' here, Link, is meant, or something. I've been getting pretty discouraged, with things seemin' to get worse all the time. Time was, the old folks say, when uffts was polite and respectful and did what they was told and took thank-you gifts and was glad to've done a human a favor. But nowadays they won't work for anybody without a agreement of just how much beer they're goin' to get for doin' it. And the old folks say there used to be unduplied cloth an' stuff that was better than we got now. And knives was better, an' tools was better, and there was lectric and machines and folks lived real comfortable. But lately it's been gettin' harder an' harder to get uffts to bring in greenstuff, an' they want more an' more beer for it. I tell you, it ain't simple, bein' a Householder these days! You got people to feed an' clothe, and the women fuss and the men get sour and the uffts set back and laugh, and make speeches to each other about how much smarter they are than us. I tell you, Link, it's time for something to happen, or things are goin' to get just so bad we can't stand them!"

The cavalcade went on, and Harl's voice continued. The

thing he deplored came out properly marshalled, and it was evident that responsibilities in an imperfect universe had caused him much grief, of which he was conscious.

Link caught an idea now and then, but most of Harl's melancholy referred to conditions Harl took as a matter of course and Link knew nothing about. For example, there was the idea that it was disgraceful to pay or be paid for anything that was done, except by uffts. On no other planet Link had heard of was commerce considered disreputable. He knew of none on which work was not supposed to be performed in exchange for wages. And there was, irrelevantly, the matter of Thistlethwaite's clothing. It was not "duplied." What was "duplied"? Everywhere, of course, the good old days are praised by those who managed to live through them. But when cloth was duplied it was inferior, and tools were inferior, and there was no more lectric—that would be electricity—and there were no more engines.

Link almost asked a question, then. The ancestors of Harl and his followers had colonized this planet from space. By spaceship. It was unthinkable that they hadn't had electricity and engines or motors. And when the way to make things is known and they are wanted, they are made! The way to make them is not forgotten! It simply isn't! But according to Harl they'd had those things and lost them. Why?

Harl murmured on, with a sort of resigned unhappiness. The state of things on Sord Three was bad. He hoped Link's arrival might help, but it didn't seem really likely. He named ways in which times had formerly been better. He named matters in which deterioration had plainly gone a long way. But he gave no clue to what made them worse, except that everything that was duplied was inferior, and everything was duplied. But what duplying was—

They passed over the top of a rolling hill. Below them the ground was disturbed. An illimitable number of burrows broke its surface, with piles of dirt and stones as

43

evidence of excavations below ground. An incredible number of pink-skinned, pig-like creatures appeared to live here.

"This," said Harl uncomfortably, "this is a ufft town. It's shortest to get back to the Household if we ride through it. They fuss a lot, but they don't ever actual do more than yell at humans goin' through. Bein' uffts, though, and knowing from those two I sent ahead that you're a stranger, they may be extra noisy just to show off."

Link shrugged.

"You fellas," said Harl sternly to his following, "don't you pay any attention to what they say! Hear me? Ignore 'em!"

The cavalcade rode down the farther hillside and entered the ufft metropolis. The splay-footed unicorns walked daintily, avoiding the innumerable holes which were exactly large enough to let full-grown uffts pop in and out with great rapidity. Had Link known prairie-dogs, he would have said that it was much like a much-enlarged prairie-dog town. The burrows were arranged absolutely without pattern, here and there and everywhere. Uffts sat in their doorways, so to speak, and regarded the animals and men with scornful disapproval. It seemed to Link that they eyed him with special attention, and not too much of cordiality.

A voice from somewhere among the burrows snapped,

"Humans! Huh! And here's a new one. Pth-th-th-th!" It was a Bronx cheer. Another voice said icily, "Thieves! Robbers! Humans!" A third voice cried shrilly, "Oppressors! Tyrants! Scoundrels!"

The six riders, including Link, gazed fixedly at the distance. They let their mounts pick their way. The scornful voices increased their clamor. Uffts—they did look astonishingly like pigs—popped out of burrows practically under the feet of the unicorns and cried out enragedly,

"That's right! That's right! Tread on us! Show the stranger! Tread on us!"

Uffts seemed to boil around the clump of unicorns. They

dived out of sight as the large splay feet of the riding-animals neared them, and then popped up immediately behind them with cries of rage, "Tyrants! Oppressors! Stranger, tell the galaxy what you see!" Then other confused shoutings, "Go ahead! Crush us! Are you ashamed to let the stranger see? It's what you want to do!"

There was a chorus of yapping ufft voices a little distance away. One of them, squatted upright, waved a fore-paw to give the cadence for choral shouts of, "Men, go home! Men, go home! Men, go home!"

Harl looked unhappily at Link.

"They never had manners, Link. But this is worse than I've seen before. Some of it's to make you think bad of us, you bein' a stranger. I'm right sorry, Link."

"Humans seem pretty unpopular," said Link. "They aren't afraid of you, though."

"I can't afford to be hard on 'em," admitted Harl. "I need 'em to bring in greenstuff. They know it. They work when they feel like they want some beer. They get enough beer for a party an' then they make speeches to each other about how grand they are an' how stupid us humans are. If I was to try to make 'em act respectful, they'd go get their beer from another Household, an' we wouldn't have any greenstuff brought in. An' they know I know it. So they get plenty fresh!"

"Yah!" rasped a voice almost underfoot. "Humans! Humans have paws! Humans have hands! Shame! Shame! Shame!"

The unicorns plodded on, their flaccid upside-down horns drooping and wabbling. They climbed over mounds of dirt and stones, and down to level ground between burrows, and then over other mounds. Their gait was incredibly ungainly. The clamor of ufft voices increased. The nearby tumult was loud enough, but the ufft city stretched for a long way. It seemed that for miles to right and left there were shrilling,

45

pink-skinned uffts galloping on their stubby legs to join in the abuse of the human party.

"Yah! Yah! Humans! Men, go home! Hide your paws, Humans!" A small group yelled in chorus, "The uffts will rise again! The uffts will rise again!" Yet another party roared, although some of the voices were squeaky, "Down with Households! Down with tyrants! Down with Humans! Up with uffts!"

The cavalcade was the center of a moving uproar. At the beginning there'd been some clear space around the feet of the unicorns. But uffts came from all directions, shrilling abuse. Swarms of rotund bodies scuttled up and over the heaps of dug-out dirt and stones, and they ran into other swarms, and they crowded each other closer to the mounted men. Some were unable to dart aside, and dived down into burrows to escape trampling. They popped out behind the unicorns to yap fresh insults. Then one popped out directly underneath a unicorn, and the unicorn's pillowy foot sent him rolling, and squealing, but unhurt, and then there was an uproar.

"Dirty humans! Tyrants! Now you kill us."

"Hold fast to your saddle, Link," said Harl bitterly. "They'll be bitin' the unicorns' feet in a minute. That'll be the devil! They'll run away and y'don't want to get thrown! Not down among them!"

Link reined aside and held up his hand for attention. He was a stranger and part of this demonstration was for him. He knew something about demonstrators. For one thing, they are always attracted, almost irresistibly, to new audiences. But there is another and profound weakness in the psychology of a mob. When it is farthest from sane behavior, it likes to be told how intelligent it is.

"My friends!" boomed Link, in a fine and oratorical carrying voice. "My friends, back at the ship I had a conversation with two of your cultured and brilliant race, which filled me

46

with even increased respect for your known intellectuality!"

There was a slight lessening of the tumult nearby. Some uffts had heard pleasing words. They listened.

"But that conversation was not necessary," Link announced splendidly, "to inform me of your brilliance. On my home planet the intellect of the uffts of Sord Three has already become a byword! When a knotty problem arises, someone is sure to say, 'Ah, if we could ask the uffts of Sord Three about this, they'd settle it!' "

The nearer uffts were definitely quieter. They shushed those just behind them. Then they shouted to Link to go on. There was still babbling and abuse, but it came from farther away.

"So I came here," Link announced in ringing tones, "to carry out a purpose which, if accomplished, will make it probable that the anniversary of my arrival will be celebrated over the entire surface of at least one planet! My friends, I call upon you to bring this about! I call upon you to cause such rejoicing as indubitably will modify the future of all intellectual activities! Which will bring about a permanent orientation ufftward of the more abstruse ratiocinations of the intellectuals of the galaxy! I call upon you, my friends, to give to other worlds the benefit of your brains!"

He paused. He knew that Harl listened with startled incomprehension. He could see out of the corner of his eyes that the other halted men were bemused and uneasy, but the uffts within hearing cheered. Those too far away to hear clearly were trying to silence those behind them. They cheered to make the balance listen. Link bowed to the applause.

"I bring you," he boomed with a fine gesture, "I bring you a philosophical problem, which is also a problem in sophistic logic, that the greatest minds of my home planet have not been able to solve! I have come to ask the uffts of Sord Three to use their superlative intellects upon this baffling intellectual question! There must be an answer! But it has eluded the greatest brains of my home system. So I ask the uffts of Sord Three to become the pedagogues of my world. You are our only hope! But I do not feel only hope! I feel confidence! I am sure that ufftian intellect will find the answer which will initiate a new era in intellectual processes!"

He paused again. There were more cheers. Much of the cheering came from uffts who cheered because other uffts were cheering.

"The problem," said Link impressively, and with ample volume, "the problem is this! You know what whiskers are. You know what shaving is. You know that a barber is a man who shaves off the whiskers of other men. Now, there is a Household in which there is a barber. He shaves everybody in the Household who does not shave himself. He does not shave anybody who does shave himself. The ineluctible problem is, who shaves the barber?"

He stopped. He looked earnestly at all parts of his audience.

"Who shaves the barber?" he repeated dramatically. "Consider this, my friends! Discuss it! It has baffled the philosophers and logicians of my home world! I have brought it to you in complete confidence that, without haste and after examining every aspect of the situation, you will penetrate its intricacies and find the one true solution! When this is done I shall return to my home world bearing the triumphant result of your cerebration and a new field of intellectual research will be opened for the minds of all future generations!"

He made a gesture of finality. There was really loud cheering now. Link was a stranger. He had flattered the uffts and those near him were charmed by his tribute, and those farther away cheered because those near him had cheered, and those still farther away—

"Let's get going," said Link briefly.

THE DUPLICATORS

The cavalcade took up its march again. But now there were groups of uffts running alongside Link's unicorn, cheering him from time to time and in between beginning to argue vociferously among themselves that the barber did or didn't shave himself because if he didn't, or if he did, why? And if he wore whiskers he would not shave himself and therefore would have to shave himself and therefore couldn't have whiskers.

The angular, ungainly unicorns moved in their slab-sided fashion across the remaining dirt piles and burrows of the ufft city. Behind them, a buzz of argument began and rose to the sky. Uffts by thousands zestfully discussed the problem of the barber. He shaved everybody who didn't shave himself. He didn't shave anybody who did shave himself. Therefore—

Harl rode in something like a brown study for a long way after the ufft metropolis was left behind. Then he said heavily,

"Uh . . . Link, did you sure-enough come here to ask the uffts that there question?"

"No," admitted Link. "But it seemed like a good idea to ask it."

Harl considered for a long time. Then he said,

"What did you come here for, Link?"

Link considered in his turn. Viewing the matter dispassionately, he didn't seem to have had any clear-cut reason. One thing had led to another, and here he was. But a serious-minded character like Harl might find the truth difficult to understand. So Link said with a fine air of regret,

"I'll tell you, Harl. There was a girl named Imogene—"

"Uh-uh," said Harl regretfully. "I'm gettin' kind of troubled about you, Link. You're guestin' with me, an' all that, but that whiskery fella that cussed so bad an' insulted me, he came on the spaceship with you. And that speech you made to those uffts—I don't understand it, Link. I just don't understand it! You seem like a right nice fella to me, but I'm a Householder and I got responsibilities. And I'm gettin' to think that with times like they are, and the uffts cheering you like they did, an' all my other troubles—"

"What?" asked Link.

"I hate to say it, Link," said Harl apologetically, "an' it may not seem mannerly of me, but honest I think I'd better get you hung along with that whiskery fella that wanted to send a message to Old Man Addison. I won't like doin' it, Link, and I hope you won't take it unkindly, but it does look like I better hang you both to avoid trouble."

Harl's followers rearranged themselves, closing Link in so there was no possibility of his escape.

◆

IV

THEY REACHED the village which Harl pointed to with the comment that it was his Household. They rode into it, and there were a good many women and girls in sight. They were elaborately clothed in garments at once incredibly brilliant and sometimes patched. But only a few men were visible. There were no dogs, such as properly belong in a small human settlement, but there were uffts in the streets sauntering about entirely at their ease. Once the cavalcade passed two of them, squatted on their haunches in the position of quadrupeds sitting down, apparently deep in satisfying conversation. It overtook a small cart loaded with a remarkable mixture of leaves, weeds, roots, grass, and all manner of similar debris. It looked like the trash from a gardening job, headed either for a compost heap or for a place where it would be burned to be gotten rid of. But there were four uffts pulling it by leather thongs they held in their teeth. It had somehow the look of a personal enterprise of the uffts, personally carried out.

A little way on there was a similar cart backed up to a wide door in the largest building of the village. That cart was empty, but a man in strikingly colored, but patched, clothing was putting plastic bottles into it. The contents looked like beer. An ufft supervised the placing, counting aloud in a sardonic voice as if ostentatiously guarding against being cheated. Three other uffts waited for the tally to be complete.

The cavalcade drew rein at a grand entrance to this largest building. Harl dismounted and said heavily,

"Here's where I live. I don't see anything else to do but hang you, Link, but there's no need to lock you up. Come along with me. My fellas will be watchin' all the doors an' windows. You can't get away, though I mighty near wish you could."

The four other riders dismounted. There'd been no obvious sign of Link's change of status, from warmly-approved guest to somebody it seemed regrettably necessary to hang, but after Harl's decision his followers had matter-of-factly taken measures to prevent his escape. There was no hope of a successful dash now, nor was there any place to dash to.

Link climbed down to the ground. During all his life, up to now, he'd craved the novel and the unexpected. But it hadn't happened that the prospect of being hanged had ever been a part of his life. In a way, without realizing it, he'd taken the state of not being hanged for granted. He'd never felt that he needed to work out solid reasons against his hanging as a project. But Harl appeared to be wholly in earnest. His air of regret about the necessity seemed sincere, and Link rather startledly believed that he needed some good arguments. He needed them both good and quick.

51

"Come inside," said Harl gloomily. "I never had anything bother me so much, Link! I don't even know what it's mannerly to do about your ship. You ain't given it to me, and you welcomed me in it, so it would be disgraceful to take it. But it's the most iron I ever did see! And things are pretty bad for iron, like most other things. I got to think things out."

Link followed him through huge, wide doors. It looked like a ceremonial entrance way. Inside there was a splendid hall hung with draperies that at some time had been impressive. They were a mass of embroidery from top to bottom and the original effect must have been one of genuine splendor. But they were ancient, now, and they showed it. At the end of the hall there was a grandiose, stately, canopied chair upon a raised dais. It looked like a chair of state. The entire effect was one of badly faded grandeur. The present effect was badly marred by electric panels which obviously didn't light, and by three uffts sprawled out and sleeping comfortably on the floor.

"Most of my fellas are away," said Harl worriedly. "An ufft came in yesterday with some bog-iron and said he'd found the biggest deposit of it that ever was found. But y'can't trust uffts! He wanted a thousand bottles of beer for showin' us where it was, and five bottles for every load we took away. So I got most of my fellas out huntin' for it themselves. The ufft'd think it was a smart trick to get a thousand bottles of beer out of me for nothing, and then laugh!"

One of the seemingly dozing uffts yawned elaborately. It was not exactly derisive, but it was not respectful, either.

Harl scowled. He led the way past the ceremonial chair and out a small-sized door just beyond. Here, abruptly, there was open air again. And here, in a space some fifty by fifty feet, there was an absolutely startling garden. It struck Link forcibly because it made him realize that at no time on the journey from the landed *Glamorgan* to the village had he seen a sign of cultivated land. There was very little vegetation of any sort. Isolated threads of green appeared here and there, perhaps, but nothing else. There'd been no fields, no crops, no growing things of any sort. There was literally no food being grown outside the village for the feeding of its inhabitants. But here, in a space less than twenty yards across, there was a ten-foot patch of wheat, and a five-foot patch of barley, and a row of root-plants which were almost certainly turnips. Every square inch was cultivated. There were rows of plants not yet identifiable. There was a rather straggly row of lettuce. It was strictly a kitchen-garden, growing foodstuffs, but on so small a scale that it wouldn't markedly improve the diet of a single small family. In one corner there was an apple tree showing some small and probably wormy apples on its branches. There was another tree not yet of an age to bear fruit, but Link did not know what it was.

And there was a girl with a watering can, carefully giving water to a row of radishes.

"Thana," said Harl, troubled. "This's Link Denham. He came down in that noise we heard a while ago. It was a spaceship. That whiskery fella came in it too. I'm goin' to have to hang Link along with him—I hate to do it, because he seems a nice fella—but I thought I'd have you talk to him beforehand. Coming from far-off, he might be able to tell you some of those things you're always wishin' you knew."

To Link he added,

"This's my sister Thana. She runs this growin' place and not many Households eat as fancy as mine does! See that apple tree?"

Link said, "Very pretty" and looked carefully at the girl. At this stage in his affairs he wasn't overlooking any bets. She'd be a pretty girl if she had a less troubled expression. But she did not smile when she looked at him.

"You'd better talk to that whiskery man," she said severely to her brother. "I had to have him put in a cage."

"Why not just have a fella watch him?" demanded Harl. "Even if a man is goin' to be hung, it ain't manners not to make him comfortable."

The girl looked at Link. She was embarrassed. She moved a little distance away. Harl went to her and she reported something in a low tone. Harl said vexedly,

"Sput! I never heard of such a thing! I . . . never . . . heard of such a thing! Link, I'm goin' to ask you to do me a favor."

Link was in a state of very considerable confusion. It seemed settled that he faced a very undesirable experience. Hanging. But he was not treated as a criminal. Harl, in fact, seemed to feel rather apologetic about it and to wish Link well in everything but continued existence. But now he returned to Link, very angry.

"I'm going to ask you, Link," he said indignantly, "to go see that whiskery fella and tell him there's a end to my patience! He insulted me, an' that's all right. He'll get hung for it and that's the end of it. But you tell him he's got to behave himself until he does get hung! When it comes to tryin' to send a message to my sister—*my sister*, Link— offerin' to pay *her* for sendin' a message to Old Man Addison, I'm not goin' to stand for it! He's gettin' hung for sayin' that to me! What more does he want?"

Link opened his mouth to suggest that perhaps Thistlethwaite wanted to get a message to Old Man Addison. But it did not seem tactful.

"You see him," said Harl wrathfully. "If I was to go I'd prob'ly have him hung right off, and all my fellas that didn't see it would think it was unmannerly of me not to wait. So you talk to him, will you?"

Link swallowed. Then he asked,

"How will I find him?"

THE DUPLICATORS

"Go in yonder," said Harl, pointing, "and ask an ufft to show you. There'll be some house-uffts around. Ask any one of 'em."

He turned back to his sister. Link headed for the pointed-out door. He heard Harl, behind him, saying angrily,

"If he don't behave himself, sput! Hangin's too good for him!"

But then Link passed through the door and heard no more. Uffts in their own village were openly derisive of Harl. But they sauntered about his house and slept on his floors and he certainly tolerated it. He found himself in a hallway with doors on either side and an unusually heavy door at the end. It occurred to him that he was nearly in the same fix as Thistlethwaite, though Thistlethwaite had wanted to send a message, while he'd only made a speech to the uffts. He groped for something that would make sense out of the situation.

An ufft slept tranquilly in the hall. It was very pig-like indeed. It looked like about a hundred-pound shote, with pinkish hide under a sparse coating of hair. Link stirred the creature with his foot. The ufft waked with a convulsive, frightened scramble of small hoofs.

"Where's the jail?" asked Link. He'd just realized that he couldn't make plans for himself alone, since Thistlethwaite was in the same fix. It made things look more difficult.

The ufft said sulkily,

"What's a jail?"

"In this case, the room where that man who's to be hung is locked up," said Link. "Where is it?"

"There isn't any," said the ufft, more sulkily than before. "And he's not locked up in a room. He's in a cage."

"Then where's the cage?"

"Around him," said the ufft with an air of extreme fretfulness. "Just because you humans have paws isn't any reason to wake people up when they're resting."

"You!" snapped Link. "Where's that cage?"

The ufft backed away affrightedly.

"Don't do that!" it protested nervously. "Don't threaten me! Don't get me upset!"

It began to back away again. Link advanced upon the ufft.

"Then tell me what I want to know!"

The ufft summoned courage. It bolted. Some distance away it halted at a branching passage to stare at Link in the same extreme unease.

"He's in the cellar," said the ufft. "Down there!"

It pointed with a fore-hoof.

"Thanks," said Link, with irony.

The ufft protested, complainingly,

"It's all very well for you to say thanks after you've scared a person."

Link moved forward, and the ufft fled. But Link's intentions were not offensive. He was simply following instructions. He moved doggedly down the hallway. It was carpeted. But the carpet was worn and frayed, though once it had been luxurious. He noted that the plastering was the work of a less than skilled workman.

He came to a corner in the hallway wall. A flight of steps went downward, to the left. He went down them. He heard voices. One of them had the quality of an ufft's speech.

"Now, we can do it. The fee will be five thousand beers."

Thistlethwaite sounded enraged.

"Outragious! Robbery! One thousand bottles!"

"Business is business," said the other voice. "Four. After all, you're a human!"

Link's foot made a scraping sound on the floor. There was an instant scuffling and low-voiced whispers and mutterings of alarm. Link went toward the sound and came to a place where a wick burned in a dish of oil. The light played upon an oversized cage of four-by-four timbers, elaborately lashed together with rope. Inside the cage, Thistle-thwaite glared toward the sound of the interruption.

Beyond the cage there was a very neat pile of vision-receivers, all seemingly new and every one dusty. The combination of unused vision-receivers and a wick floating in a disk of oil for light was startling. The light was primitive and smoky. The vision-sets were not. But the light worked and the vision-sets didn't. Evidently. There were electric-light panels. But they wouldn't work either, or the oil lamp would not exist. Thistlethwaite didn't see Link, as yet.

"You'd better tell your boss," rasped Thistlethwaite to the sound that was Link, "that if he ever expects to do any business with Old Man Addison he'd better let me loose and give me back my clothes and—"

He stopped short. He and Link could see each other now. Thistlethwaite was bare and hairy and caged. At sight of Link he uttered a bellow of rage through the heavy wooden bars.

"You!" he roared. "What' you doin' here? I told you to keep ship! You go back there! You want the ship to be claimed as jetsam, an abandoned ship with no representative of the owner on board? You get there! Lock y'self in! You stay on board till I finish my business dealin' and come an' tell you what to do next!"

"There's someone in charge," said Link mildly. "One of Harl's retainers is acting as watchman. For me. There've been developments since then, but that's that about the ship. I've got a message for you from Harl."

Thistlethwaite sputtered naughty words in naughtier combinations.

"It seems," said Link, "that to offer to pay a Householder for something is insult amounting to a crime. That's what you're to be hung for. Offering to pay a Householder's sister for something is a worse crime. It appears that doing business, except with uffts, is considered disgraceful. I don't see how they make it work, but there you are. If you'll apologize, I think there's a chance."

Thistlethwaite cried out, furiously,

"How can you do business without doin' business? You go tell him—"

"I'd like to get you off," said Link mildly. "I'm supposed to be hanged, too. But if I get you a pardon I might get one for myself as a particept noncriminus. So—"

He heard faint sounds. He said,

"If you've a better way of getting out of being hanged than apologizing, I'd like to join you. I have an idea that there are persons of larger views than . . . ah . . . the humans on Sord Three. I refer to that brilliantly intellectual race, the uffts. With their cooperation—"

He definitely heard faint sounds. There had been voices before he arrived at Thistlethwaite's cage. He waited hopefully.

"Look here!" snapped Thistlethwaite, "I'm the senior partner in this business! You signed a contract leavin' all decisions to me an' you doin' only astrogatin'! You leave this kinda business to me! I'll tend to it!"

There was a slight scraping noise. An ufft came out from behind the pile of vision-sets. Other uffts appeared from other places. The first ufft said,

"You said you are to be hanged. Would you be interested in a deal with us? We can do all sorts of jail-deliveries, strikes, sabotage, spying and intelligence work, and we specialize in political demonstrations." The ufft grew enthusiastic. "How about a public demonstration against hanging visitors from other worlds? Mobs shouting in the streets! Pickets around the Householder's home! Chanted slogans! Marching students! And demonstrators lying on the ground and daring men to ride unicorns over them! We can—"

"Can you guarantee results?" asked Link politely.

"It'll be known all over the planet!" said the ufft proudly.

"Public opinion will be mobilized! There'll probably be sympathetic demonstrations at other Households. There'll be indignation, meetings! There'll be petitions! There'll be—"

"But what," asked Link as politely as before, "just what will be the actual physical result? Will Thistlethwaite be released? And I'm supposed to be hanged too. Will I be pardoned? What will Harl actually do in response to all these demonstrations?"

"His name will go down in history as among the most despicable of all tyrants who tried to keep us uffts in bondage!"

"Not in human histories," said Link. "Not in histories written by men! Actually, Harl will go his placid way and hang Thistlethwaite and me. And I hate to say it, but our ghosts won't get the least bit of comfort out of even the most violent of public reactions after the event."

The ufft made no reply.

"I have a thought," said Link. "Everybody has a weakness. You have yours, Harl has his, I have mine. Harl's is that he is hell on manners. Fix things so he'll be unmannerly if he doesn't pardon both of us, and he'll be like putty. If Thistlethwaite apologizes elaborately enough, pleading ignorance of the local customs—"

Thistlethwaite protested bitterly,

"Apologize for a straight business proposal? A sound business transaction? I offered to pay him liberal—"

"Exactly the point," said Link. "Exactly!"

"Mobs in the streets, shouting to shame him," said the first ufft, enthusiastically. "Pickets around his house, chanting slogans! Uffts lying in the streets, daring men to ride over them."

"No," said Link patiently. "Thistlethwaite apologizes. He didn't know the local customs. He asks Harl to forgive him and permit him to make a guest-gift of the clothes and the stun rifle Harl has already taken. No expense there! Then he asks Harl to instruct me in local etiquette so he can observe it in future contacts with Harl, whom he hopes to make his guide, mentor, friend, and most intimate companion when he has made himself worthy of Harl's friendship."

"I won't do it!" raged Thistlethwaite ferociously. "I won't do it! I'm goin' to run this in a businesslike way! That ain't business!"

"It's sense," observed Link.

"You're fired!" bellowed Thistlethwaite. "You're fired! You ain't a junior partner any more! Your contract with me says I can heave you out any time I want! You're heaved! I'm runnin' this my way!"

Link looked at him earnestly, but the little man glared furiously at him. Link shrugged and went away. He returned to the garden, where Harl paced up and down and up and down, and where his sister again watered a row of not over-prosperous plants.

"Thistlethwaite," said Link untruthfully, "had an unhappy childhood, practically surrounded by people with the manners, morals, and many of the customs of uffts. It warped his whole personality. He is aware that he ought to apologize for having insulted you. But he's ashamed. He feels that he should be punished. Also he feels that he should make reparation. At the moment he is struggling between a death-wish and an inferiority complex. He will offer no more insults unless the struggle goes the wrong way."

Harl scowled.

"But there is a reasonable probability," added Link, "that he will end up by making the spaceship and its cargo his guest-gift to you. That would get you out of an unpleasant dilemma. It would be very mannerly to accept it. You'd have the ship and your manners in getting it would be above reproach."

Harl said suspiciously,

"How much time is he likely to take?"

"When were you planning to hang us?" asked Link.

"After the fellas get back," said Harl. "They may be a while having their suppers. Then I was figurin' we'd have the hangin' by torch-light. It'll make a right interestin' spectable, flamin' torches an' such and a hangin' by their light. My fellas will talk about it for years!"

"Just take it easy," advised Link. "Don't hurry things. He'll come around before anybody gets too sleepy to appreciate his hanging!"

He hoped it was true. It ought to be. But Harl paced up and down.

"I wouldn't want to do anything unmannerly," he said grudgingly. "All right. I'll give him until hangin' time." Then he seemed to rouse himself. "Thana, you pick the stuff for supper and I'll get it duplied while you ask Link questions about the things you want to know."

The girl plucked half a dozen lettuce plants. A handful of peas. She examined the apples on the tree and picked one. It was a small and scrawny apple. Link saw a worm-hole near its stem. She handed the vegetation to her brother. Then she said to Link,

"I'll show you."

He followed her. She went into the building, and they were in the great hall with the canopied chair. She led the way across the hall and into a smaller room. It was lined with shelves, and ranged upon them were all the objects a Householder could desire or feel called on to supply to his retainers. There were shelves of tools, but only one of each. There were shelves of cloth. Much of it was incredibly beautiful embroidery, but it was age-yellowed and old. There were knives of various shapes and sizes, plates, dishes, and glassware, bits of small hardware, and sandals, purses, and neckerchiefs, although these last categories were in poor condition indeed. In general, there was every artifact of a culture which had made vision-sets and now was used floating wicks in oil for illumination.

Link suddenly knew that this was in a sense the treasury of the Household. But there was only one of each object on display.

Thana pulled out a drawer and showed Link an assortment of rocks and stones of every imaginable variety. She searched his expression and said,

"When you make a stew, you put in meat and flour and what vegetables you have. That's right, isn't it?"

"I suppose so," agreed Link. He was baffled again by his surroundings and, of all possible openings for a conversation, the subject she'd just mentioned.

"But," said Thana uncomfortably, "it doesn't taste very good unless you put in salt and herbs. That's right too, isn't it?"

"I'm sure it is," said Link. "But—"

"Here's a knife." It was in the drawer with the rocks. She handed it to him. It was a perfectly ordinary knife; good steel, of a more or less antique shape, with a mended handle. It had probably had a handle of bone or plastic which by some accident had been destroyed, so someone had painstakingly fitted a new one of wood. She reached to a shelf and picked up another knife. She handed it to Link, too.

He looked at the pair of them, at first puzzled and then incredulous. They were identical. They were really identical! They were identical as Link had never seen two objects before. There was a scratch on the handle of each. The scratches were identical. There was a partly broken rivet in one, and the same rivet was partly broken in precisely the same fashion in the other. The resemblance was microscopically exact! Link went to a window to examine them again, and the grain of the wooden handles had the same pattern, the same sequence of growth-rings, and there was a jagged nick in one blade, and a precise duplicate of that nick in the other. Perhaps it was the wood that most bewildered Link. No two pieces of wood are ever exactly alike. It can't happen. But here it had.

"This knife is duplied from that," said Thana. "This one is duplied. That one isn't. The unduplied one is better. It's sharper and stays sharper. Its edge doesn't turn. I . . ." She hesitated a moment, "I've been wondering if it isn't something like a stew. Maybe the unduplied knife has something in it like salt, that's been left out of the duplied one. Maybe we didn't give it something it needs, like salt. Could that be so?"

Link gaped at her. She didn't looked troubled now. She looked appealing and anxious and—when she didn't look troubled she was a very pretty girl. He noticed that even in this moment of astonishment. Because he began to make a very wild guess at what might explain human society on Sord Three.

His limited experience with it was baffling. From the moment when he sat on the exit port threshold of the *Glamorgan* and chatted with an invisible conversationalist, to the moment he'd been told regretfully by Harl that he'd have to be hanged because of a speech he'd made about a barber, every single happening had confused him. It seemed that beer was currency. It seemed that a fifty-foot-square garden somehow supplied food for an entire village, though its plants seemed quite ordinary. Right now, dazedly surveying the whole experience, he recalled that there was no highway leading to the village. No road. It was not irrelevant. It fitted into the preposterous entire pattern.

"Wait a minute!" said Link, astounded and still unbelieving. "When you duply something you . . . furnish a sample and the material for it to something and it . . . duplicates the sample?"

"Of course," said Thana. Her forehead wrinkled a little as she watched his expression. "I want to know if the reason

63

some duplied things aren't as good as unduplied ones is that we leave something out of the material we give the duplier to duply unduplied things with."

His expression did not satisfy her.

"Of course if the sample is poor, the duplied thing will be poor quality too. That's why our cloth is so weak. The samples are all old and brittle and weak. So duplied cloth is brittle and weak too. But," she asked unbelievingly, "don't you have dupliers where you come from?"

Link swallowed. If what Thana said was true—*if* it was true—an enormous number of things fell into place, including Thistlethwaite's scornful conviction that wealth in carynths was garbage compared with the wealth that could be had from one trading-voyage to Sord Three. If what Thana said was true, that was true, too. But there were other consequences. If dupliers were exported from Sord Three, the civilization of the galaxy could collapse. There was no commerce, no business on Sord Three. Naturally! Why should anybody manufacture or grow anything if raw material could be supplied and an existent specimen exactly reproduced. What price riches, manufactures, crops, . . . civilization itself? What price anything?

Here, the price was manners. If someone admired something you owned, you gave it to him, it or a duplied, microscopically accurate replica. Or maybe you kept the replica and gave him the original. It didn't matter. They'd be the same! But the rest of the galaxy wouldn't find it easy to practise manners, after scores of thousands of years of rude and uncouth habits.

"Don't they have dupliers where you come from?" repeated Thana. She was astonished at the very idea.

"N-no," said Link, dry-throated. "N-no, we d-don't."

"But you poor things!" said Thana commiseratingly. "How do you live?"

THE DUPLICATORS

For the first time in his life, Link was actually terrified. He said the first thing that came into his mind.

"We don't," he said thinly. "At least, we won't live long after we get dupliers!"

V

THERE WAS movement in the great hall next door, but Thana paid no attention. She put one knife back on the shelf from which she'd taken it. She began to show Link the collection of small rocks and stones she'd accumulated.

"Here's a piece of rock we call bog-iron," she said absorbedly. "It has iron in it. Put this rock, with some wood, in the duplier, and a sample knife for it to duply, and the duplier takes iron out of the bog-iron and wood out of the wood and makes another knife. Of course the rock crumbles because part of it has been taken away. So does the wood, for the same reason. But then we have another knife. Only it's only so good. So I thought that if an unduplied knife has something besides iron in it, like a stew has salt, maybe if I found the right kind of rock the duplier would take something out of it, and if it was the right kind of . . . of whatever-it-is, the duplied knife would be as good as the original because it had everything in it the original knife had."

"Yes," said Link, still dizzy. "It would. It should. If you get the right kind of rock."

"Do you know what kind that would be?" asked Thana eagerly. "Can you show me the right kind?"

Link shook his head.

65

"Not I," he said wrily. "It's a special profession to know what rocks are ores and which aren't. Some of these rocks I do recognize. That blue one may have copper in it. I've seen it but I'm not sure. This pink one I know. I spent months digging it out in mountain-size masses, looking for a place where a meteor might have struck it on a world where they used to have severe meteor-showers. But the rest, no."

She looked distressed.

"Then there's not much use in having guessed something right, is there? When you go away in your spaceship could you send somebdy back who does know about rocks? We might even have lectric again!"

"I'm supposed to be hung," said Link more wrily still. "And even if I could, I don't think I'd do it. Because he'd go away again and tell the outside worlds that you have dupliers on Sord Three. And men would come here to take them away from you. They'd rob you at least, more likely murder you to get your dupliers and then they'd take them and destroy themselves."

He made a rather absurd gesture. When one had been raised in a galaxy where every world has its own government, but they are so far apart that they can't fight each other, patriotism as loyalty to a given place or planet tends to die out. It has no function. It serves no purpose. But Link knew now that when men no longer cherished small nations, whether they knew it or not they were loyal to mankind. And dupliers released to mankind would amount to treason.

If there can be a device which performs every sort of work a world wants done, then those who first have that instrument are rich beyond the dreams of anything but pride. But pride will make riches a drug upon the market. Men will no longer work, because there is no need for their work. Men will starve because there is no longer any need to provide them with food. There will be no way to earn necessities. One can only take them. And presently nobody will attempt to provide them to be taken.

Thana said interestedly,

"There are stories about the fighting back on Suheil Two before our ancestors ran away. Everybody was trying to kill them because they had dupliers. They had to flee. It seems ridiculous, but they did run away, in spaceships, and they came here. There were only a few hundreds of them. The uffts made quite a fuss about their setting up Households, but the men had beer and the uffts couldn't make it. They had no hands. So things got straightened out in time. But for a long, long while it was believed that nobody from any other world must ever be allowed to land here. I'm glad you landed, though."

"To be hanged," said Link.

But he understood the history of Sord Three better than she did. He could imagine the Economic Wars on Suheil Two, after the ancestors of Thana had fled. There were dupliers that weren't taken away by the fugitives. A few. So men fought to possess them, and other men fought to take them away, and ultimately they'd be destroyed by men who couldn't defend them. And then there'd be wholesale murder for food, and brigandage for what scraps were left. And at last civilization would have to start all over again with starving people and unplanted fields for a beginning. But no dupliers.

Here the disaster had taken a different form. While dupliers worked there was no need to learn useful things, such as the mechanical arts, and chemistry, and minerology. So such knowledge was forgotten. The art of weaving would vanish, too, when dupliers could make cloth to any demand. The composition of alloys. Electrical apparatus could not work without rare metals nobody knew how to find for the dupliers. So when the original units wore out there was no more electricity. And all cloth grows old and yellow and brittle, so old cloth, duplied, merely meant more old cloth, and alloy steel objects could not be reproduced, but only duplied, without the alloying materials, so there were only soft-iron knives and patched garments. And since the smallest of gardens, with any kind of vegetable matter for raw material, could have its produce duplied without limit, only the smallest of gardens were cultivated. Wherefore Harl's Household was hung with rich drapery which was falling apart, the carpets on its floors were threadbare, and he was proud that his Household had one scrawny apple tree with wormy fruit on it. Because on Sord Three men were not needed to make things or grow things or do things. And Harl's Household was ready to break apart.

"I begin," said Link unhappily, "to agree with Harl. Since Thistlethwaite can't hope to astrogate his ship if I'm hanged, he can't report the state of things without me. So it's probably wise to hang me. On the other hand I couldn't run the ship's engines, so I couldn't take the news if he were hanged. But one or the other of us should be disposed of."

Thana said sympathetically, `

"You feel terrible, don't you? Let's go see Harl. Maybe you'll feel better. No, wait!" An idea had occurred to her. She surveyed a shelf of elaborately embroidered garments. She picked out one. "Do you think this is pretty?"

"Very," said Link forlornly. There hadn't been too many things he'd taken seriously, in his lifetime, but he did know that if dupliers got loose in the galaxy, there'd be no man certain of his life if he hadn't a duplier, nor any man whose life was worth a pebble if he did.

"Fine!" said Thana brightly. "Come along!"

She picked up a bundle of what looked like ancient, yellowed, cloth scraps, plus a lump of bog-iron. She led the way into the great hall.

Her brother Harl was there, wearing an expression of patient gloom. There were two retainers, working at something which gradually became clear. A third man rolled in a large wheeled box from somewhere. It was filled to the brim with a confused mass of leaves and roots and branches and weeds. It was the mixture uffts had been dragging into the village in a wheeled cart some little while ago. As a mixture, it belonged on a compost-heap or on a brush-pile to be burned. But instead it was brought into the hall with the incredible, falling-apart, floor-to-ceiling draperies.

There was a stirring. The dais and the canopied chair moved. Together, chair and dais rose ceilingward. A deep pit was revealed where they had stood. And something rose in the pit, like a freight-elevator. It came plainly into view, and it was a complex metal contrivance with three hoppers on top which were plainly meant to hold things. One of the hoppers contained a damp mass of greenish powder in a highly ir-regular mound. One of Harl's retainers began to brush that out into a box for waste. The middle hopper contained a pile of apples, all small, all scrawny, and each with a wormhole next its stem. It contained a bushel or more of lettuce heaped up with the apples. The rest of the hopper was filled with peas.

The third of the hoppers contained an exact duplicate of the contents of the middle hopper. Each leaf of lettuce in the third hopper was a duplicate of one in the middle hopper. Each apple was a duplicate of an apple in the mid-dle hopper. Each pea—

"Pyramid it once more," said Harl, "and it'll be enough."

His retainers piled the contents of the third hopper into the second. They piled the first one high with the contents of the box of vegetable debris. Link knew the theory now. The trash was vegetation. There were the same elements and same compounds in the trash as in apples, lettuce leaves, and peas. The proportions would be different, but the substance would be there. The duplier would take from the trash the materials needed to duplicate the sample edibles.

The same thing could more or less be done with roasts and steaks. Or elaborate embroidery, provided one had a sample for the duplier to work from. There would be left-over raw materials, of course, but a duplier could duplicate anything. Including a duplier.

And that was the thought which was frightening.

Harl said,

"All right."

The men moved back. The contrivance descended into the pit. The chair of state descended until its dais rested on the floor, covering the pit. Harl said casually,

"How'd you make out, Thana? Does Link know some of the things you were wonderin' about?"

"Most of them," said Thana confidently. "Nearly all!"

It was less than an accurate statement, and Link wondered morosely why she made it. But then Harl pressed the button. The chair of state rose. The deep pit was revealed. The metal contrivance rose to floor-level. The pile of assorted fragments in the first hopper had practically vanished. The fruit and lettuce and peas in the second hopper were unchanged. The third hopper was full of an exact duplicate of the assortment of edibles in the middle one.

"We don't need any more," observed Harl. "Just clean up and—"

"Wait!" said Thana. "I was showing Link things, and he admired this shirt."

She unfolded the garment she'd asked Link's opinion on. It was a shirt. It was lavishly embroidered. Link opened his mouth, but Harl said indulgently,

"All right."

Thana put the shirt in the middle—sample—hopper. Then she said,

"He told me the knife you've got is the prettiest he's seen, too!"

Harl said, "Sput!" His tone was not entirely pleased. Then he said, "I got to have manners, huh?"

"Of course," said Thana.

With a grimace, Harl unbuckled his belt and handed the belt and knife to Thana. She put them into the middle hopper. Then she put bog-iron, wood, and the scraps of cloth from the treasury room into the raw materials place. She nodded confidently to her brother.

He pressed something, the chair of state sank down, following the duplier mechanism, the room looked normal for a moment, and then the chair of state rose up, the pit appeared, and then the duplier.

There was much less bog-iron in the materials hopper. There was some sand on the hopper bottom. The embroidered shirt and the knife and belt were, as they'd been before, in the middle hopper. Exact duplicates of both knife and shirt were in the third hopper.

Thana handed her brother his knife. She took out and put aside the sample garment. She spread out its duplicate and said to Link,

"Do put it on! Please!"

Harl watched imaptiently, as Link took off his own shirt and donned the embroidered one. He was embarrassed by his own decorative appearance in the new apparel. Thana picked up the shirt he'd taken off.

"Look! This is unduplied, Harl!" she said with extravagant admiration. "Have you ever seen anything so wonderful?"

"Sput!" said Harl angrily. "What you tryin' to do?"

"I'm saying that this is a wonderful shirt," said Thana, beaming. "It isn't duplied. It's the nicest, newest shirt I've ever seen. Don't you think so? I dare you to lie and still pretend you've manners!"

Harl said, "Sput!" again, and then,

"All right," he admitted peevishly. "It's true. I never saw a new, unduplied shirt before. It's a nice shirt."

71

Thana turned triumphantly to Link. He didn't see any reason for triumph. But she waited, and waited. Harl glared at him. Suddenly, Link understood. He might be scheduled to hang, but he was expected to be mannerly.

"The shirt is yours," he said dourly to Harl. "It's a gift."

Harl hesitated for what seemed a long time. Then,

"Thanks," he said reluctantly. "It's a right nice guest-gift. I appreciate it."

Thana looked radiant. She sent one of the retainers, standing by, for all the cloth on the treasury room shelves. She fairly glowed with enthusiasm. She put Link's former shirt in the sample hopper and filled another with scraps, and sent the duplier down. It came up and there were two shirts. It went down again with two shirts in the sample hopper. When it came up there were four. The chair of state and the duplier went down and up and down and up and down and up. When the last morsel of raw material was exhausted, there were one hundred twenty-seven duplicates of Link's own shirt, besides the original shirt itself.

"I guess that'll do," said Harl, ungraciously. "I'll be sendin' gifts to all my friends, and all my own fellas will have new shirts, an' their wives'll be takin' 'em apart to make dresses and sheets and stuff." He nodded to Link. "I appreciate that shirt a lot, Link. Thanks."

He went away, and Link stirred stiffly. He'd watched the entire process. Objects could be duplicated without labor or skill or industry. He'd observed what his mind told him was the doom of human civilization unless he or Thistlethwaite were hung. Or both. But now he saw something more. Even that would not preserve the galaxy from destroying itself by riches out of dupliers. Eventually, certainly, another ship must land on Sord Three. It might be by accident. But some day another ship would come. And then this same intolerable situation would exist again.

"I'll see about dinner now," said Thana. She turned warm, grateful, admiring eyes upon Link, and vanished.

Harl shook his head as she disappeared.

"Smart girl, that! I wouldn't ha' thought of usin' manners to get your shirt off your back so's I could admire it and have the first new cloth since the old days! Mighty smart girl, Link!"

Link said stiffly,

"If you're through with taking my shirt in vain, what now?"

Harl looked surprised.

"Oh, you go off somewheres and set down and rest yourself, Link," he said kindly. "I got things to do. Excuse me!"

He departed. Link was left alone in the great hall, morbidly weighing the alternatives, himself or Thistlethwaite or both of them hanged against the collapse of all the economy of all the galaxy, with wars, murders, lootings and rapine as a necessary consequence. He didn't have to ask what Thistlethwaite had planned to trade for, on Sord Three. It was dupliers. And dupliers could obviously duplicate each other as well as more commonplace objects. Thistlethwaite wanted to make contact with Old Man Addison to trade unduplied objects for dupliers. Old Man Addison was evidently so disreputable a Householder that he would do business, if tempted. He'd provide a shipload of dupliers, especially duplied for the off-planet trade, in exchange for objects that dupliers couldn't duplicate on Sord Three. It would seem to him an excellent bargain.

It would seem an excellent bargain to business men elsewhere, too, to pay a hundred million credits and half the profits for a duplier. Thistlethwaite was right. Carynths were garbage in comparative value. A business man could begin with the luxury trade and undersell all other supplies, dispensing duplied luxury items. Then he could undersell any manufacturer of any other line of goods. He could undersell

73

normally grown foodstuffs. Any supplier of meat products. Any supplier of anything else men needed or desired. All factories would become unprofitable. They'd close. All working men would become unemployed. All wages would cease to move except into a duplier-owner's pockets. And then there would be disaster, calamity, collapse, destruction, and hell to pay generally.

And Thistlethwaite couldn't foresee it. He was incapable of looking beyond an immediate, enormously profitable deal.

Link scowled. He alone could envision the coming disaster. He alone could think of measures to prevent it. And he was supposed to be hanged presently for a speech about an imaginary barber! It was wrong! It was monstrous! He had to stay alive to save the galaxy from the otherwise inevitable!

There was an ufft seemingly asleep in the far corner of the hall. As Link approached, the ufft opened its eyes.

"Why didn't you tell Harl you admired Thana when he said she was a smart girl?"

The ufft had evidently been eavesdropping. It occurred to Link that there probably weren't many human secrets unknown to the uffts. They lounged about the village streets and they casually napped or seemed to doze in the Householder's home itself.

"Why should I say that?" asked Link irritably.

"If you want to marry her," said the ufft, "that's the start of it."

"But I just met her!" said Link.

The ufft stirred, in a manner suggesting a shrug by a four-footed animal lying prone on the floor.

"And what are you going to do about Thistlethwaite?" the ufft demanded. "He's going to escape. It's all arranged. Three thousand bottles of beer, payable by written contract when he gets to Old Man Addison's. But he's mad with you. He says you're not part of his organization any

74

more. You're fired for disobeying orders to stay in the ship. He says he got you for an astrogator—what's an astrogator?—because he couldn't get anybody better. He says he can astrogate the ship to where he wants to go by doing everything you did, backwards." Link thought sulfurous thoughts. The ufft went on, "He says he and Old Man Addison will make history on Sord Three. Why is Sord Three Sord Three? Why not just Sord?"

"Sord's the sun," said Link grimly, thinking of something else. "This is the third world from it."

"That's silly!" said the ufft. "What did you come here for, anyway? What did you expect to get out of it?"

"In spite," said Link, "of the remarkable similarity between your interrogation and those of other individuals with equally dubious justification, I merely observe that my motivation is only to be revealed to properly constituted authorities, and refrain from telling you to go fly a kite."

"What's a kite?" asked the ufft.

Link said,

"Look! I'm supposed to be hung presently. I disapprove of the idea. How about arranging for me to escape along with Thistlethwaite?"

The ufft said,

"Five thousand beers?"

"I haven't got them," admitted Link.

"Three? Will Old Man Addison pay them for you?"

"I've never met him," said Link.

"What else have you to offer, then?" asked the ufft in a businesslike tone. "I have to get a commission, of course."

"I made a speech in the ufft city," said Link hopefully, "on the way here from the ship. It was very well received. I may have some . . . hm . . . friends among my listeners who would think it unfortunate if I were hanged."

The ufft got to its four feet. It stretched itself. It yawned. Then it said,

"Too bad!"

It trotted out of the hall.

Link found himself angry. In fact, he raged. Thistleth-waite, if he escaped, might actually try to astrogate the *Glamorgan* back to Trent by the careful notes Link had made in the ship's log. It wasn't too likely he'd manage it, but it was possible. If he did, then Link would have died in vain. He went storming about the building. He hadn't realized it, but it was now near sunset and what of the sky could be seen through windows was a flaming, crimson red. He came upon an ufft sauntering at ease from one room to another, and a second settling down for a tranquil nap. But he saw no human until he blundered into what must be a kitchen. There Thana bustled about in what must once have been a completely electrified kitchen, now with lamps which were simply floating wicks for illumination. There were two retainer-girls assisting her. They used the former equipment as tables, and the cooking was done over a fire of dried-out leaves and twigs.

"Oh," said Thana cordially. "Hello."

"Listen!" said Link, "I want to make a protest!"

"I'm terribly busy," said Thana pleasantly, "and anyhow Harl's the one to tell about anything that's missing in the treatment of a guest. Would you excuse me?"

Link changed his approach.

"I've got an idea," he said rather desperately. "I think I know how to identify the kind of . . . of salt you want to add to bog-iron to make good knives from your unduplied sample."

"For that!" said Thana warmly, "I'll stop cooking! What is it, Link?"

"When you put bog-iron in the duplier," said Link har-assedly, "and the duplier makes a knife, the bog-iron crumbles because the iron's been taken away." Link was irritated, now. "The idea is to make a series of knives, adding different rock-samples to each one, until you get a good knife. Then the rock that contained the alloy-metal you wanted will be crumbled like the iron. See?"

"Wonderful!" said Thana, pleased. "I should have thought of it! I'll try it tomorrow!"

There was a faint noise outside. It was a shrill, ululating sound. Link paid no attention. Instead, he said urgently,

"And I think I can work out some ways that might get electricity back!"

"That would be marvelous," said Thana. "You must tell Harl what they are! At dinner, Link. Tell him about them at dinner. He's busy now, arranging about the torchlight for the hanging. But I thank you very kindly for telling me the trick to make better knives. I'm sure it will work! But I really do have to get dinner ready!"

The noise outside grew louder. There were shouts. It sounded like a first-class riot beginning. Thana tilted her head on one side, listening.

"The uffts are putting on a demonstration," she said without particular interest. "Why don't you go watch it, Link? You can tell Harl all your new ideas when we have dinner! I think it's wonderful of you to think of things like this! You've no idea how important it will be! Excuse me now?"

She bustled away. Link ground his teeth. If Thistlethwaite escaped, he must, too. Thistlethwaite might carry out the bargain with Old Man Addison and try to astrogate back to Trent. The emergency wasn't that he might not make it, but that he might.

Link made his way in the general direction of the tumult. It was dark inside the big building, now. Once away from the feeble oil-wick lamps, he seemed merely to run into walls and partly-opened doors and heavy, misplaced furniture. Once he heard a heavy clattering of small hoofs indoors, somewhere inside the building. A remarkable number of uffts seemed to be racing madly up stairs and down a hallway to the open air. The sound of their hoofs changed as they went out-of-doors. The noises from outside changed as they left the door open behind them. Link had heard only the back-ground noise, a continual shrill yapping, but now he heard individual voices.

"Down with humans! Down With the Murderers of Inter-stellar Travelers! Uffts forever! Men go home!" There was a particularly loud outburst. *"We want freedom! We want freedom!"* Then a squealing from a myriad voices from small pig-like throats. *"Yah! Yah! Yah! Men have hands! Yah! Yah! Yah!"*

Link reached the open door. Darkness had fallen with the suddenness only observable in the tropics of some ten thousand planets. It occurred to him that the troop of uffts he'd heard in the building was probably Thistlethwaite's special rescue squad. If they'd had to rush past or through a human guard at the doorway, such a guard would now be in poor condition to resist his own exit. And it was dark and there was enough confusion to cover one man, even a man supposed to be hung, while he left the householder's residence.

He was right. Starlight showed hundreds of small, rotund bodies galloping madly up and down the street, shrilling squealed insults at the human race in general and Harl in particular. There was one especial focus of tumult. Three men on unicorns were its center. They were apparently Harl's retainers returning from a hunt for an alleged new deposit of bog-iron. They'd been caught in the village street by the suddenly erupting disorder. They were surrounded by uffts, running around them like a merry-go-round, squealing denunciations at the tops of their voices.

"Men have hands. Shame! Shame! Shame! Down with murderers of interstellar travelers! Uffts forever! Down with men! Down—"

The retainers' ungainly mounts tried to find a way through the squealing mob of uffts. But they were timorous. They lifted their large splay feet with a certain fearful suddenness and put them down with an attempt at delicacy. They managed to make their way along the ufft-covered street until they were almost opposite the doorway in which Link waited for a chance to leave without being instantly bowled over.

Then a unicorn made a misstep. A foot came down on an ufft. The galloping small animal squealed, *"He tramped on me!"* and ran away shrieking its complaint.

The sound of uproar doubled. Link went out into the darkness, to escape. He saw torches burning where men were at work building something which was plainly a gallows. Until this instant they had taken the noise and galloping calmly. They'd continued to work, though from time to time they looked with mild interest at the milling, racing small creatures which raced up and down the street, making all the noise they possibly could.

But the stepped-on shrieking ufft, complaining to high heaven of the indignity put upon him, which did not lessen his speed or his voice, changed everything. Uffts came swarming more thickly than ever about the mounted men. They seemed to climb over each other to get closer to the unicorns and squeal more ferociously than before.

And the unicorns panicked. Link saw a huge, pillowy forefoot lift with an ufft clinging to it, biting viciously. The ufft let go and bounced off its fellows on the ground. Other uffts bit at the unicorns' feet. One of them went down to its knees and its rider toppled off. The three awkward animals bolted. All three fled crazily from the village with gigantic, splay-footed strides. The man who'd been thrown was buried under squealing uffts, while the greater number of the demonstrators went galloping after the runaway unicorns. The riders of two unicorns tried frantically to control them, but the saddle of the third was empty.

Link heard the covered-up man swearing blood-curdlingly.

He found himself plunging toward his fellow-human. Quite automatically, his hands grasped two ufftian hind-legs and threw two uffts away over the heads of their fellows. Two more. Two more. Squealings from the thrown uffts seemed suddenly to terrify those who had been most valiant and most vocal in the attack.

Link again threw away two more and two more still, and suddenly the creatures were running insanely in all directions. Some ran between his legs in wild, shrill terror. They jammed that opening and Link went down with a crash, still hanging on to a kicking hindleg. The man he'd come to rescue continued to swear, now without uffts to muffle his words, which were remarkable. And there were men running to the scene with torches.

Link let go of the ufft he held captive. He had to, to get up. The ufft went streaking for the far horizon at the top of his voice. Harl came out of the Household, fuming.

"Sput!" he fumed. "Those uffts! They bit through the lashin's of that whiskery man's cage an' let him loose! All this fuss was gettin' him escaped! Sput! I was figurin' on havin' a real spectacular hangin'! An' he's got away!"

The man to whose rescue Link had gone now got to his feet. He spoke, with a depth of feeling and aptness of expression that put Harl's indignation in the shade. His garments were shreds. He'd been nipped at until he was practically nude. The arriving torches even showed places where blood flowed from deeper nips than usual.

"And it was goin' to be a swell hangin'," mourned Harl indignantly. "Torchlight an' stuff! I was just waitin' for all the fellas to get back, and the fella had to escape! But there's—"

He stared.

"Link!"

VI

"THIS," SAID LINK, at once with dignity and with passion, "this is no time to be fooling around with hangings!"

Harl blinked at him in the starlight.

"What's the matter, Link? What' you doin' outside the house? That fella got away, but there's—"

"Me, yes!" snapped Link. "But we can't spare the time for that now! Get some men mounted! We've got to catch Thistlethwaite!"

"We don't know where he went," objected Harl.

"I do!" Link snapped at him. "He went to the ship! If for nothing else, to get some pants! Then he'll go to Old Man Addison's. The uffts'll take him. He'll make a business deal with him! A trade! A bargain!"

It was an absurd time and place for an argument. Men with torches lighted one small part of the street. They'd come to help a fellow-human momentarily buried under swarming, squealing uffts. Link had gotten there first. Then Harl. Now Link, with clenched fists, faced Harl in a sort of passionate frustration.

"Don't you see?" he demanded fiercely. "He was on Sord Three last year! He made a deal with Old Man Addison then! He's brought a shipload of unduplied stuff to trade with Old Man Addison for dupliers! Don't you see?"

Harl wrinkled his forehead.

"But that'd be . . . that wouldn't be mannerly!" he objected. "That'd be—sput, Link! That'd be . . . business!"

He used the term as if it were one only to be used in

81

strictly private consultation with a physician, as if it were a euphemism for something unspeakable.

"That's exactly what it is!" rasped Link. "Business! And bad business at that! He'll sell the contents of his ship to Old Man Addison and be paid in dupliers! And with the dupliers—"

"Sput!" Harl waved his hands. He bellowed, "Everybody out! Big trouble! Everybody out! Bring y'spears!"

Men came out of houses. Some of them wore shirts such as Link wore no longer. They were pleased with them. Since the article duplicated was relatively new, the replicas of it had all the properties of new shirts, though the raw stuff of the thread involved had previously had the properties of the centuries-old sample from which it had been duplied, and which hadn't been new since before the art of weaving was forgotten. New-shirted retainers came out of houses to hear Link's commands.

"Get mounted!" roared Harl. "We' ridin' to that ship that come down today. What's in it's goin' to Old Man Addison if we don't get there first! Take y'spears! Get movin'! The uffts are goin' too far!"

There was confusion. More men appeared and ran out of sight. Some of them came back riding unicorns. Some led them. The three animals that had been ringed in and whose tender feet had been bitten by the uffts now came limping back into the village. The two riders had somehow managed to subdue their own beasts, and then had overtaken and caught the riderless animal.

"A unicorn for Link!" roared Harl, in what he evidently considered a military manner. "Get him a spear!"

"Hold it!" said Link grimly. "That stun-gun you took from Thistlethwaite! You were carrying it. I'll take that, Harl! I know how to use it!"

"I ain't had time to figure it out," said Harl, agreeing.

He roared. "Get that funny dinkus the whiskery man was carryin' this mornin'! Give it to Link!"

Confusion developed further. Since his first sight of Harl, riding up to the ship with five unicorn-mounted men at his back, Link had made innumerable guesses about the social and economic system of Sord Three. Most of them had been wrong. He'd been sure, though, that the organization into Households was a revival or reinvention of a feudal system, in which a Householder was responsible for the feeding and clothing of his retainers, and in return had an indefinite amount of power. Harl had the power, certainly, to order strangers hung.

But it became clear that whether it was feudal or not, the system was not designed for warfare. Harl was in command, but nobody else had secondary rank. There were no under-officers or non-commissioned ones. Harl's howled and bellowed orders got a troop of mounted men assembled. Confusedly and raggedly, they grouped themselves. They carried spears and wore large knives. Harl bellowed additional orders and whoever heard them obeyed them more or less. With great confusion, the group of armed and mounted men got ready to start out in the moonlight.

Just as he was about to give the order to march, Thana's voice came from the building which was the Householder's residence.

"Harl! Harl! If you go off now, dinner will get cold!"

"Let it!" snapped Harl. "We got to catch that whiskery fella!"

He roared for his followers to march, and march they did in a straggling column behind him. Somebody confusedly searched for and found Link, riding next to Harl, to give him the stun gun which was the only weapon that had been aboard the *Glamorgan*. He felt it over in the darkness.

"It seems to be in working order," he told Harl. "Thanks."

"What—" Then Harl saw the stun gun. The starlight was

moderately bright, but it was not possible to see the details of anything, whether of the armed party or the landscape. "Oh. You got that thing. I was layin' off to figure out what it was, but I didn't have time. What's it do, Link?"

"It knocks a man or an animal out," said Link curtly. "It shoots an electric charge. But you can set the charge not to stun him, but only sting him up more or less."

" 'Lectric?" asked Harl. "That's interestin'! How far does it throw?"

"That depends," said Link.

"Mmmmm. Uh, Link, how did you find out that that whiskery fella is makin' a deal with Old Man Addison?"

"Uffts told me," said Link grimly. "Old Man Addison is going to pay three thousand bottles of beer for Thistle-thwaite's delivery to him. It's a written contract. Thistle-thwaite wouldn't promise anything like that if he didn't know his value to Old Man Addison!"

Harl shook his head.

"You spoiled a good hangin' by not tellin' me!" he said reproachfully. "He got away. But how d'you know he's head-in' for the ship?"

"I told you!" said Link. "He wants pants. He wants a shirt. He wants clothes. He wants to be dressed like a business man when he does business with Old Man Addison!"

Harl considered.

"It looks reasonable," he admitted. "Right reasonable!"

"I was offered a deal to escape, too," said Link sourly. "The uffts wanted five thousand bottles of beer to take me to Old Man Addison's Household."

"You wouldn't like him," said Harl sagely. "He's hardly got any more manners than an ufft. Anybody who's mannerly like you are couldn't get along with him, Link. You showed sense in stayin' with me."

"To be hanged!" said Link bitterly. "But—"

"Hold on!" said Harl in astonishment. "Didn't I admire

that shirt o' yours? An' didn't I accept it as a gift? I could make a gift to a man I was goin' to hang, Link. That'd be just manners! But I couldn't accept a gift an' then hang him! That'd be disgraceful!" He paused and said in an injured tone, "I've heard of Old Man Addison doin' things like that, but I never thought anybody'd suspect it of me!"

Link waved his hand impatiently. It was remarkable that the discovery that plans for his hanging were changed should make so little difference in this thinking. But right now he was concerned with the prevention of a disaster vastly more important than any concern of his own.

"I doubt," he said, "that we'd better go through the ufft city. We'd better circle it. We'd be delayed at best, and Thistlethwaite is in a hurry to settle his bargain with Old Man Addison. He'll hurry."

Harl cleared his throat and bellowed toward the skies. The trailing cavalcade of ungainly unicorns changed direction to follow him.

The mounted party was probably fifty men and animals strong. In the dimness of starlight alone, it was an extraordinary sight. The men rode in clumps of two or three or half a dozen, on steeds whose gait was camel-like and awkward. The unicorns wabbled as they strode. Their limp and fleshy horns swayed and swung. Link, looking back and observing the total lack of discipline, felt an enormous exasperation.

He didn't like the situation he was in, even when immediate hanging was no longer included. In all his life before he'd been carefree and zestfully concerned only with doing things because they were novel or exciting, and on occasion because they involved some tumult. In anybody his age, that was a completely normal trait. But now he had a responsibility of intolerable importance. The future of very many millions of human beings would depend on what he did, but he'd get no thanks for his trouble. It went against the grain of Link's entire nature to dedicate himself to a tedious and exacting task like this. If he were successful it would never be known. In fact, it was a condition of success that it must never be known anywhere off of Sord Three. And it mustn't be understood there!

At least an hour after their starting out a high, shrill clamor set up, very far away.

"That's uffts," said Harl. "Somethin's happened an' they feel all happy an' excited."

"It's Thistlethwaite," said Link. "He got to the ship. He probably passed out some gifts to the uffts."

The cavalcade went on. The faint shrill clamor continued.

"Uh, Link," said Harl, in a tone at once apologetic and depressed, "I thought of somethin' that might make the uffts feel good. If like you said he gave presents to the uffts, maybe it was unduplied things. They couldn't use 'em, havin' hoofs instead of hands. But they'd know us humans 'ud have to buy 'em. They like to bargain. They enjoy makin' humans pay too much. It makes 'em feel smart and superior. He could ha' made a lot of trouble for us humans! A lot o' trouble!"

The long, somehow lumpy line of men and animals went on through the darkness. Harl said unhappily,

"The uffts were tryin' to make me pay 'em for news of where there was a lot of bog-iron. You figure what they'd make me pay for somethin' unduplied! If that fella's passin' out that kinda gifts, the uffts feel swell. They feel happy. But I don't!"

Link said nothing. It would be reasonable for Thistlethwaite to feel that he had to get samples of his cargo aground to ensure his deal with Old Man Addison, and then to have a train of armed men and animals come to unload the *Glamorgan* and carry its specially purchased cargo away. If he opened a cargo-compartment to get samples, the uffts could well have demanded samples for themselves. Or they could simply take them.

"And," Harl fumed, "when they got something they'll ask fifty bottles of beer for, they won't bother bringin' in greenstuff, and how'll I get the beer to pay 'em? They'll bring in knives an' cloth and demand beer! And if I don't have the beer, they'll take the stuff to another Household."

"Then you'll probably have to pay it."

"Without greenstuff, I can't," said Harl bitterly.

There was an addition to the faint, joyous clamor beyond the horizon. Link began to discount any chance of success in this expedition. If Harl was right, Thistlethwaite had gotten to the ship, had gotten more clothing, and had very probably passed out in lieu of cash or beer, such objects of *virtu* as mirrors, cosmetics, cooking pots made of other metals than iron, crockery, small electric appliances like flashlights, pens, pencils, and synthetic fabrics. None of these things could be duplied on Sord Three, because the minerals required as raw materials had been forgotten if they were ever known.

And all this would put Harl in a bad situation, no doubt. Every Householder would need to deal with Old Man Addison for such trinkets, which he must supply to his retainers or seem less than a desirable feudal superior. But to Link the grim fact was that Thistlethwaite must have gotten to the ship before the mounted party. If he suspected pursuit he'd waste no time. He'd go on. And if he had gone on—

Dead ahead, now, there were peculiar small sounds. It took Link seconds to realize that it was the hoofs of uffts on metal stair-treads and metal floors, the sound coming out of an opened exit port.

"Harl," said Link in a low tone, "Thistlethwaite may still be in the ship. There are certainly plenty of uffts rummaging around in there! Can you get your men—"

But Harl did not wait for such advice as a self-appointed chief of staff might give to his commander-in-chief on the eve of battle. He raised his voice,

"There they are, boys!", he bellowed. "Come along an' get 'em! Get the whiskery fella! If we don't get him there'll be no hangin' tonight!"

Roaring impressively, he urged his awkward mount forward. He was followed by all his undisciplined troop. It was a wild and furious and completely confused charge. Link and Harl led it, of course. They topped a natural rise in the ground and saw the tall shape of the *Glamorgan* against the stars.

There was a wild stirring of what seemed to be hordes of uffts, clustered about the exit port and swarming in and swarming out again. A light inside the port cast an inadequate glow outside and in that dim light, rotund, piglike shapes could be seen squirming and struggling to get into the ship, if they were outside, or to get out if they happened to be in. Link saw the glitter of that light upon metal. Evidently the uffts were making free with at least the contents of one cargo compartment. They were bringing out what small objects they could carry.

Harl bellowed again, and his followers dutifully yelled behind him, and the whole pack of them went sweeping over the hillcrest and down upon the aggregation of uffts. The unicorns were apparently blessed with good night-vision, because none of them fell among the boulders that strewed the hillside.

The charge was discovered. Squeals and squeaks of alarm came from the uffts. It was not as much of a tumult as so many small creatures should make, however. Those with aluminum pots and pans, or kitchen appliances, or small tools or other booty, those of them with objects carried in their mouths simply bolted off into the dark, making no outcry because it would have made them drop their loot. Link saw one of them with an especially large pot dive into it and roll over, and pick it up again and run ten paces and then trip and dive into it again before it found a way to hold the pot safely and go galloping madly away.

The other uffts scattered. But there were boulders here. They shrilled defiant slogans from behind them. *"Down with men! Uffts forever!"* They yapped at the men on their unicorns. So far as combat was concerned, however, the charge on the spaceship was anticlimactic. The uffts outside either fled with whatever they'd picked up in their teeth, or scattered to abuse the men from lurking-places among the boulders all round about. But there were very many more inside the ship. They came streaming out in a struggling, squabbling flood. The riders did not try to stop them. They seemed satisfied and even pleased with themselves over the panicky flight of the uffts. They clustered about the exit port, but they allowed the uffts through as they fled.

"What'll we do now?" asked Harl.

"See if Thistlethwaite's inside," said Link curtly.

He got the stun gun ready. There'd been no effort by any of the riders to use their spears on the uffts. Link could understand it. Uffts talked. And a man can kill a dangerous animal, or even a merely annoying one, but it would seem like murder to use a deadly weapon on a creature which was apparently incapable of anything more dangerous than nipping at a unicorn's foot or tearing the clothes of a man buried under a squealing heap of them. A man simply wouldn't think of killing a talking animal which couldn't harm him save by abuse.

Harl swung from his saddle and strode inside the ship. Link heard him climb the metal stairs inside. There was a wild squealing sound, and something came falling down the steps with a clatter as of tinware. An ufft rolled out of the door and streaked for the horizon, squealing.

There were more yellings.

"Down with murderers of interstellar travelers!" squeaked an invisible ufft somewhere nearby. *"Men have hands!*

Shame! Shame! Shame!" yapped another. Then a chorus set up, *"Men go home! Men go home! Men go home!"*

The men on the unicorns seemed to grow uneasy. They were bunched around the exit port of the ship. There were very many uffts concealed nearby. They made a racket of abuse. Sometimes they shouted whatever of competing out-cries caught their fancy, as in the rhythmic, "Men go home!" effort. Then there was merely a wild clamor until some especially strident voice began a more attractive phrase of insulting content.

There were thumpings inside the ship. Harl bellowed some-where. More thumpings. The yellings of abuse grew louder and louder. Apparently the burdenless uffts had ceased to flee when they found themselves not pursued. The torrent of insult became deafening. At the very farthest limit of the light from the port, round bodies could be seen, running among the boulders as they yelled epithets.

The riders stirred apprehensively. The military tactics of the uffts, it could be said, consisted of derogatory outcries for moral effect and the biting of unicorns' feet as direct attack. Agitated running in circles had prefaced the attack on three unicorns, most tender parts in the village street. The riders in the starlight, here, were held immobile because Harl was inside the ship. But they showed disturbance at the prospect of another such attack on their mounts. More, there came encouraging, blood-thirsty cries from across the hilltop as if a war party from the ufft city were on the way to reinforce the uffts making a tumult about the ship.

Footsteps. Two pairs of them. Harl came out the exit port, very angry, with a woe-begone retainer following him.

"This fella," said Harl, fuming, "is the one I left to watch the ship for you, Link. The whiskery fella came here with a crowd of uffts. He hadn't any clothes on and he told this fella he'd got in trouble and needed to get his clothes. The fella thought it was only mannerly to let a man have his own clothes, so he let him in. An' then the whiskery fella hit him from behind with somethin', an' locked him in a cabin an' let the uffts in."

Link said curtly,

"Too bad, but—"

"We'd better get movin'," said Harl angrily. "We missed him. He musta got away before we found it out. He opened up a door somewheres, this fella says, and he heard him cussin' the uffts like they were just takin' anything they could close their teeth on. Then he heard some noise."

An ufft leaped a boulder and darted at the uneasily stamping unicorns. He hadn't quite the nerve to make it all the way. He swerved back. But other uffts made similar short rushes. Presently there'd be one underfoot, nipping at the animals' feet, and they'd stampede.

"We'd better get movin'," said Harl. "They're gettin' nervy."

"No," said Link, grimly. "Wait a minute!"

He swung the stun gun around. He opened the cone-of-fire aperture. He adjusted the intensity-of-shock stud. He raised it. The yells were truly deafening. "Scoundrels! Villains" yapped the racing, jumping small creatures.

Link pulled the trigger. The stun gun made a burping noise. Electric charges sped out of it, scattering. The gun would carry nearly a hundred yards at widest dispersion of its fire. Within the cone-shaped space it affected, any flesh unshielded by metal would receive a sharp and painful but totally uninjurious electric shock. To men who knew nothing of electricity it would have been startling. To uffts it would be unparalleled and utterly horrifying. They squealed.

Link fired it again, at another area in the darkness. Shrieks of ufftian terror rose to the stars.

"Murderers!" cried ufft voices. "Murderers! You're killing us!"

Link aimed at the voices and fired again. Twice.

The uffts around the spaceship went away from there, making an hysterical outcry in which complaints that the complainer had been killed were only drowned out by louder squealings to the effect that the squealers were dead.

"Sput!" said Harl, astounded. "What're you doin', Link? You ain't killin' 'em, are you? I need 'em to bring in green-stuff!"

"They'll live," said Link. "Wait here. I want to see what Thistlethwaite did. Anyhow he didn't try to lift the ship off to Old Man Addison's Household!"

He went in. He climbed the stairway. He saw a cargo compartment door. It had been sealed. It was now welded shut. Thistlethwaite had used an oxygen torch on it. A second cargo door. Welded shut. The third door was open. It was apparently the compartment from which the loot of the uffts had come. It appeared to be empty. The engine room door was welded shut, and the spaceboat blister. The control room was sealed off from any entry by anybody without at least a cold chisel, but preferably a torch. And the oxygen torch was gone.

Link went down the stairs again, muttering. Thistlethwaite had made the *Glamorgan* useless to anybody possessing neither a cold chisel nor an oxygen torch. Harl couldn't seize the materials Thistlethwaite planned to trade for dup-liers. Old Man Addison might—

In the one gutted cargo space—he looked into it again with no hope at all—he found a plastic can of beans, toppled on the floor. He picked it up. It was too large for the jaws of uffts to grasp.

He went down to the exit port again, piously turning out the electric lights that Thistlethwaite had left burning. He was deeply and savagely disappointed. He was almost at the exit port when an idea came to him. He climbed back up and touched the bottom-most weld. It scorched his fingers.

Thistlethwaite hadn't done it long ago. He couldn't be far off.

Link turned on the lights again and searched. The only loose object left anywhere was an open can of seal-off compound, for stopping air-leaks such as the *Glamorgan* had a habit of developing. It was black and tarry and even an ufft would not want it. Link did.

He reached the open air again. He said briefly,

"Hold this, Harl."

He handed over the container of beans and worked on the landing fin in which the exit port existed. He had only the narrow bristle brush used to apply the seal-off compound, and only the compound to apply. The light was starlight alone. But when he'd finished he read the straggling letters of the message with some satisfaction. The message read:

"THISTLETHWAITE,

HOUSEHOLDERS DELIGHTED WITH TEST OF WEAPONS TO MAKE UFFTS WORK WITHOUT PAY. LEAD YOUR GANG INTO AMBUSH AS PLANNED FOR LARGE SCALE USE OF WEAPON. WATCH OUT FOR LINK. HE IS PRO-UFFT AND SECRETLY AN UFFT SYMPATHIZER.

"What'd you do, Link?" demanded Harl. "The uffts've all run away, squealing. What'd you do? And what's that writing for?"

"That writing," said Link, "is to end the Thistlethwaite problem on Sord Three. You may not realize that there is such a problem, Harl, but that's to take care of it. And what I did was use a stun gun at maximum dispersion and minimum power. And I'm going to ask you, Harl, to go back to the Household straight through the ufft city. If they try to object I'll give them more of what they've had. I think the psychological effect will be salutary."

Harl thought it over. His followers did not look very military in the starlight.

"Wel-l-l-l," said Harl, "I'm not sure what those words

93

THE DUPLICATORS

mean, Link, but I was thinkin' we'd have a tough time gettin' home, with uffts bitin' the unicorns' feet all the way. But you say we won't. Or do you?"

"Yes," said Link. "I say we won't. I guarantee it."

"Then we'll try it," said Harl heavily. "Uh . . . what's this you gave me to hold?"

"It's a guest-gift for Thana," said Link.

Harl bellowed.

"Come on, fellas! Back to home! We're ridin' through the ufft city! There's a dinkus with maximum dispersion an' minimum power that drove off the uffts just now, an' we want to use it on them some more."

The cavalcade set out upon another long, shambling journey underneath the stars. It was some time before the unicorns reached the ufft city. It was not silent, even though all was darkness. There were shrill babblings everywhere. The agitated stories of uffts who'd experienced stun gun stings were being discussed by uffts who hadn't experienced them. Those who'd felt the shocks couldn't describe them, and those who hadn't couldn't believe them. The discussions tended to grow acrimonious. Then there were squealings that men were about to pass through the city. Those who hadn't been shocked went valiantly to oppose the passage, or at least make it as unpleasant as possible by abuse.

Link let the congregation of zestfully vituperative uffts grow very large and get very near. *"Murderers!"* and *"Massacrers!"* were the least of the epithets thrown at the men. *"The world will hear of this massacre!"* shouted an ufft. Another took it up, *"They'll know how many of our comrades you murdered tonight!"* The unicorns picked their way onward in their loose-jointed, wabbling fashion. Voices found an easier word. *"Killers!"* they shouted from the darkness. *"Killers! Killers!"* Actually, and Link knew it, no ufft in all the city would be able to find so much as a spot on his hide that was pinker than the rest, come tomorrow morning.

94

But now— Presently there was a huge, milling, madly galloping and wildly yelling barrier of uffts before the cavalcade. If the animals went into it, their feet would suffer. They'd be bitten. If they turned back, the uffts would be encouraged to follow and close in on them and again bite large splay feet.

Harl bellowed a halt. The cavalcade came to a standstill. Link gave the running, tumbling aggregation of abusive creatures two more shots from the stun gun. Individuals suffered the equivalent of bee-stings for the fraction of a second. They shrieked and ran away.

The rest of the travel through the city was without incident, save that very occasionally very brave uffts squealed insults from not less than half a mile away, and then fled still farther from the shambling line of mounts and men.

Then there were the undulating miles beyond, to where very faint and feeble lights showed through the darkness. And then eventually the houses of the village loomed up on either side.

Thana welcomed Harl and Link, but she was inclined to be distressed that their dinner now had to be warmed over and was inferior in quality for that reason. They dined. Link presented Thana with the plastic can of beans. Harl asked what they were. When Link told him, he said absorbedly,

"I've heard that there's a Household over past Old Man Addison that has beans. But I never tasted 'em myself. We'll duply some an' have 'em for breakfast. Right?"

And Link was ushered into a guest-room, with a light consisting of a wick floating in a dish of oil. He slept soundly, until an hour after sunrise. Then he was waked by the sound of shoutings. He could see nothing from his window, so he dressed and went leisurely to see from the street.

There were many villagers out-of-doors, staring at the distance. From time to time they shouted encouragement. Link saw what they shouted at.

95

THE DUPLICATORS

A small, hairy figure, chastely clad in a red-checked table-cloth around his middle, ran madly toward the Household. The figure was Thistlethwaite. The red-checked cloth had once been draped over a table in the *Glamorgan*'s mess room. Thistlethwaite ran like a deer and behind him came uffts yapping insults and trying to nip his heels.

He reached safety and the uffts drew off, shouting *"Traitor!"* and *"Murderer!"* as the mildest of accusations. But now and then one roared shrilly at him. *"Agent provocateur!"*

VII

THE SITUATION developed in a strictly logical fashion. The uffts remained at a distance, shouting insults and abuse at all the humans in the village which was Harl's Household. Hours passed. No small, ufft-drawn carts came in bringing loads of roots, barks, herbs, berries, blossoms and flowers. Normally they were brought in for the duplier to convert in part to beer, with added moisture, and in part into such items as slightly wormy apples, legumes like peas, and discouraged succulents like lettuce. There were all sorts of foodstuffs duplied with the same ufft-cart loads of material, of course. Wheat, and even flour, could be synthesized by the duplier from the assorted compounds in the vegetation the carts contained. Radishes could be multiplied. Every product of Thana's garden could be increased indefinitely. But this morning no raw material for beer or victuals appeared. The uffts remained at a distance, shrilling insults.

Thistlethwaite revealed the background events behind this development. He'd escaped from the Household, surrounded by a scurrying guard of uffts, while the political demonstration in the street was at its height. That tumult continued while he was hurried to the ufft city. There he was feted, but not fed. The uffts did not make use of human food. They were herbivorous and had no provisions for him. But they did make speeches about his escape.

He stood it so long, but he was a business man. He wanted food and he wanted clothing and he wanted to get to Old Man Addison's Household to proceed with his business deal to end all business deals. He did not think of it in such accurate terms. But he insisted on being taken first to the *Glamorgan* for food and clothing. He spoke with pride of his talent for business. The uffts mentioned, as business men, that the contract for his rescue and escort did not include food, clothing, or a trip west of the ufft city. There would be a slight extra charge. He was indignant, but he agreed.

He'd been taken to the ship. The watchman left by Harl admitted him. He overpowered that watchman and put him in a cabin for crew members. He stuffed himself, because food was more urgent than clothing. He admitted uffts, because they were clamoring below. They wanted the extra fees they'd charged him. They announced that they were not interested in human artifacts. They wanted the usual currency, beer. The whiskery man didn't have it. They suggested that they would accept cargo at a proper discount. The discount was for the fact that they'd have to trade human goods to humans for the beer they preferred. The discount would be great.

Thistlethwaite had to yield, though he raged. He opened a cargo compartment and the uffts began to empty it. Thistlethwaite wept with fury because circumstances had put him at the mercy of the uffts. In business matters they were businesslike. They didn't have any mercy. He was expressing his indignation at their attitude when they spoke

97

of demurrage to be paid for the delay he was causing. Strangling upon his wrath, he took measures. He was still taking measures when the expedition of men and unicorns charged down into the hollow where the *Glamorgan* rested. Thistlethwaite got out among the first, and was well away before the stun gun was put into use. And then, back in the ufft city, the uffts demanded compensation for the injury of an exaggerated number of their fellows in his employ.

Telling about it later, even returned to Harl's Household and presumably the prospect of being hanged, even later Thistlethwaite purpled with fury over the ufft demands. They'd have stripped him of all the *Glamorgan*'s cargo if not the ship itself, and he'd have reached Old Man Addison without a smidgin of trade-goods with which to deal. His entire journey would have been in vain. It was even unlikely that Old Man Addison would pay for his delivery, when he had nothing to offer that feudal chieftain in the way of trade.

Listening to the account, Harl said safely,

"Uffts haven't got any manners. You shoulda known better then to deal with them! You did right to come back." Then something occurred to him. "Why'd they chase you?"

Thistlethwaite turned burning, bloodshot eyes upon Link.

"Somebody," he said balefully, "somebody painted a note on the *Glamorgan*'s fin. It was addressed to me! So the uffts read it an' it said I'd brought guns for Householders to use on uffts to make 'em work for free! And the note said for me to lead the uffts into a ambush as previous arranged so's they'd get shot up! So they decided that me gettin' put in a cage an' gettin' them to escape me was a trick so's you'd get a chance to try out that stun gun on 'em last night!"

Link said mildly,

"Now, I wonder who could have done such a thing!"

Thistlethwaite strangled on his fury. He was speechless.

THE DUPLICATORS

"It begins to look," said Link with the same mildness, "like the uffts are really wrought up. I doubt that they're hanging around the Household just for the pleasure of calling us names. What do you think they want, Harl?"

"Plenty!" said Harl gloomily. "Plenty!"

"I suggest," said Link, "that you find out."

"Might as well," said Harl, more gloomily still. "If they don't bring in greenstuff, we don't eat. You can't duply what Thana grows unless you've got something to duply it with!"

He rose and went morosely out of the room where the conference had taken place. Thistlethwaite said bitterly,

"I'd ha' done better if I'd astrogated here myself!"

"Question," said Link. "You say the uffts believe you brought guns for them to be enslaved with. Did you?"

"No!" snapped Thistlethwaite.

"Did the uffts mention me?" asked Link.

Thistlethwaite practically foamed at the mouth.

"They said y'were their friend!" he raged. "They said—"

"I made them a speech," said Link modestly. "It was about a barber who shaved everybody in his village who didn't shave himself, and didn't shave anybody who did shave himself. There's been some trouble deciding who shaved the barber. They may like me for that."

Thistlethwaite made incoherent noises.

"Tut tut!" said Link. "There's one more question, but you haven't got the answer to it. I'll get Thana to help me find it out. I don't think you'll run away to the uffts again, and I don't *think* they'll hang you before I have a chance to protest. I shall hope not, anyhow."

He went in search of Thana. He found her ruefully regarding the plants in her kitchen-garden.

"There's not been an ufft-cart of greenstuff come in to-day!" she told Link unhappily, "and the uffts are shouting such bad language I don't know when they'll start bringing carts in again!"

"You've got food stored ahead?" asked Link.

"Not much," admitted Thana. "The uffts always bring in greenstuff, so there's been no need to store food."

Link shook his head.

"It looks bad," he observed. "Will you duply that gun I used last night and see if it works? It might be a solution to the problem. An unwelcome solution, but still a solution."

"Of course!" said Thana.

She led the way. To the great hall and across it, and into the room with innumerable shelves that served the purpose of a treasury. She lifted down the stun gun from a high shelf, which Link realized no uffts with hoofs instead of hands could ever climb to. She gave Link some large lumps of bog-iron. She brought out a ready-cut billet of wood.

Into the great hall again. She pressed a button and the chair of state and its dais rose ceilingward. The contrivance which was the duplier came up out of the pit the chair and dais ordinarily covered. Thana put the bog-iron and the wood in the raw-material hopper. She put the stun gun in the hopper holding the object to be duplicated. She left the third hopper empty. The duplicate to be produced should appear there.

She pressed the button. The duplier descended. The chair of state came down. She pressed the button again. The chair of state went up and the duplier arose, at a different rate of rising. The bog-iron in the first hopper was visibly diminished and there was much sand on the hopper bottom. The sample, authentic, original stun gun remained where it had been placed, in the middle hopper. But a seemingly exact duplicate remained in the last hopper.

Link took the duplied object. He examined it. He aimed it skyward and pulled the trigger. Nothing happened, not even the slight hiccough which accompanies a stun gun's operation.

He twisted the disassembly screw and the gun opened up for inspection. Link looked, and shook his head.

"No transistors," he reported regretfully. "They're made of germanium and stuff, rare metals at the best of times. We haven't any. So the gun is incomplete. A duplied stun gun needs germanium and without it it's no good, just like a duplied knife. No dice. I'm very glad of it."

Harl came in, indignant.

"Link!" he said in a tone expressing something like shock at something appalling and outrage at something crushing, "I sent a coupla fellas to find out what the uffts wanted, and the uffts chased 'em back!"

"Did they mention their reason?" asked Link.

"They yelled I was a conspirator. They yelled that the whiskery man was goin' to lead 'em into a ambush last night to be massacred. They yelled I was goin' to try to make 'em work all the time without payin' 'em beer! They yelled down with me. Me!" said Harl incredulously. "They said they were makin' a general strike against me! No greenstuff! No carrying messages from me to anywhere! No anything! I got to get rid of the thing they say killed 'em by hundreds last night. Did it kill 'em, Link?"

"Not a one," said Link. "They got stung a bit, but that's all. Nothing worse than a sting for the fraction of a second."

"They say," finished Harl astonishedly, "that the strike keeps up till I hang the whiskery fella and get rid of the gun that was used on 'em, an' let uffts search the whole Household to see if there are any more, an' repeat that search any time they please! They got to read all messages to me from anybody else, and from me to anybody! And I got to give 'em four more bottles of beer for each cartload of greenstuff they bring in from now on!"

Link considered for a moment. Then he said,

"What have you decided?"

"I couldn't if I wanted to!" said Harl. "Sput, Link! If I

hung that whiskery fella because the uffts wanted it, I'd be disgraced! Not a fella in the Household would stay here! If I let the uffts search anybody's house any time they wanted, not a woman would let her husband stay! If I agreed to that, Link, there wouldn't be a livin' soul here by sundown!"

Link somehow felt relieved. The human economy here on Sord Three had defects, even to his tolerant eyes. The humans were utterly dependent upon the uffts for the food they ate and the clothes they wore, in the sense that they depended on ufft-cart loads of raw material. At any time the uffts could shut down and starve out a human household. It was a relief to discover that humans would not submit.

"What'll you do?"

"Send a messenger to my next neighbor," said Harl angrily. "I'll say I'm comin' guestin'. I'll take half a dozen men an' forty or fifty unicorns. I'll go to his household. I'll make him a guest-gift of a duplied new shirt and a duplied can of beans. Then he can have all the shirts an' beans he wants from now on. Thats' a right grand gift, Link! So he'll be anxious to make a mannerly host-gift to me. So I'll admire how much ready-duplied food he has stored away. So he'll duply enough food to load up my train of unicorns and I'll bring it back here!"

"And then what? Suppose the uffts stage a political demonstration in the street while you're gone?"

Harl scowled.

"They better not!" he said darkly. "They . . . uh . . . they'd better not! I'll go send my messenger."

He hurried away.

Thana said,

"You don't think that's going to work out."

"It might," said Link. "But it needn't."

Thana said in a practical tone of voice,

"Let's see what we can do with that unduplied knife, Link."

THE DUPLICATORS

She went into the room Link considered the Household treasury. She came back with the alloy-steel knife, of which duplied copies so far had been only soft iron. She had her collection of variegated rocks.

She duplied the knife with bog-iron alone in the raw materials hopper. The contrivance went down in the pit, the canopied chair descended and covered the pit, then rose again and the contrivance came up once more. There was a second knife in the products hopper. She handed it to Link. He tested its edge. It turned immediately. It was soft iron. He handed it back. She cleaned out the materials hopper of sand and bog-iron, and put the just-duplied, soft-iron knife in for raw material. She added a dozen of the stones and pebbles of which some might be ores.

The duplier descended and rose. The knife had again been duplied. Its edge was still useless. The duplier had not been able to extract from the rock samples the alloying elements the original knife contained in addition to iron, and which a true duplicate would have to contain. They weren't in the rocks. Thana cleared out the useless rock specimens with a professional air.

"I'm afraid you're right, Link, about the uffts."

"How?" asked Link.

"Harl thinks about manners all the time. He's not practical, like you."

"I've never been accused of being practical before," said Link drily.

Thana put the re-duplied knife in the materials hopper. She added more rocks. When the chair descended she said,

"What did you do with yourself before you came here, Link?"

"Oh, I went hither and yon," said Link, "and did this and that."

The chair rose and the duplier reappeared. There was again another knife. It, also, was soft-iron. Thana cleared

103

away these unsatisfactory rock samples also. She shifted the soft-iron knife to the first hopper and put in more pebbles. When the duplier went down and came up again, the re-re-duplied knife had vanished from the materials hopper and reappeared in the third hopper where duplied products did appear. There was no crumbling among the pebbles which might be ores. She replaced them with still others and the duplication cycle began again.

"Where's your home, Link?"

"Anywhere," said Link. He watched the duplier descend and the chair-of-state come down to cover the pit. It rose again to disclose a re-re-re-duplicated knife. This time, too, the edge was not good. She substituted still other pebbles and sent the duplier down to do its duplying all over again.

"Where's anywhere?" asked Thana. She looked at him intently.

He told her. As the duplier went through the process of making and re-making the knife according to the provided sample, but without the alloy-material that would turn it to steel, he answered seemingly idle questions and presently was more or less sketching out the story of his life. He told her about Glaeth. He told her about his two years at the Merchant Space Academy on Malibu. He found himself saying,

"That's where I met Imogene."

"Your girlfriend?" asked Thana with possibly exaggerated casualness.

"No," said Link. "Oh, for a while I suppose you'd say she was. I wanted to marry her. I don't know why. It seemed like a good idea at the time. But she asked me business-like questions about did I have any property anywhere and what were my prospects, and so on. She said we were congenial enough, but marriage was a girl's career and one had to know all the facts before deciding anything so important. Very pretty girl, though," said Link.

Thana removed the assortment of stones that still again

had been proved to contain no metaliferous steel-hardening alloy. She put in more. Among the ones to be tested this time there was a sample of a peach-colored rock he'd noted earlier as familiar. Link stiffened for a moment. Then he reached inside his shirt and into a pocket of his stake-belt. By feeling only, he selected a small, gritty crystal. He placed it beside the sample knife.

The dais and the chair-of-state descended. He waited for it to rise up again.

"What happened?" asked Thana. Again she was unconvincingly casual.

"Oh," said Link, "I went back to where I was lodging and counted up my assets. I'd been toying with the idea of going to Glaeth to get rich. I had enough for that and about two thousand credits over. So I bought the necessary tickets and stuff, and reserved a place on a spaceship leaving that afternoon. Then I went to a florist."

Thana said blankly,

"Why?"

"I wanted to put her on ice."

The duplier came up. An irregular lump of grayish-black rock had visibly disintegrated. It was not all gone, but a good tenth of its substance had disappeared. There were glittering scales to prove its crumbling. The peach-colored stone had dropped a fine dust, too.

"This looks promising!" said Link.

He tested the edge of the duplied knife. It was excellent, equivalent to the original. It should have been. Tungsten steel does take a good edge, and hold it, too. He handed the knife to Thana, and fumbled in the bottom of the product hopper. There was a small, very bright crystal there. He picked it up, together with the other sample crystal from his stake-belt.

Very, very calmly he put two gritty crystals into the stake-belt pocket from which he'd extracted one. Thana held the duplied but this time tungsten-steel knife. She should have been enraptured. But instead she asked, almost urgently,

"Why did you go to a florist?"

"I bought two thousand credits worth of flowers," said Link. "I ordered them delivered to Imogene. They'd fill every room in her parents' home with some left over to hang out the windows. I wrote a note with them, bidding her goodbye."

Thana stared at him with a remarkable amount of interest.

"She wanted a rich husband and I hated to disappoint her," he explained. "And also, there was a chance that I might get rich on Glaeth. So I told her in my note that my multi-millionaire father had consented for me to roam the galaxy until I could find a girl who would love me for myself alone, not knowing of his millions. And I'd found her. And she was the only woman I could ever love. It was a fairly long note," Link added.

"But . . . but—"

"I said I was going away for a year to see if I could live without her. If I couldn't—even though she considered my father's millions—I'd come back and sadly ask her to marry me though my father's millions counted. If I could, I said, I'd spend the rest of my life exploring strange planets and brooding because the one woman I could love could not love me for myself, as I loved her. A very nice piece of romantic literature."

Thana said blankly,

"Then what?"

Harl appeared for the second time in the doorway. He was enraged. His hands were clenched. He scowled formidably.

"They wouldn't let my fella ride through," he said in an ominous tone. "They bit his unicorn's heels. They'd ha' pulled it down and him too! So he came back. Uffts never

dared try a trick like that before! Not in this household!
An' they never will again!"

"What—"

"I'm going to duply that gun you used last night, Link,"
said Harl ferociously, "and me and a bunch of my fellas will
go out an' sting them up like you did, only plenty! When
uffts say a man's got to be hung and a householder can't
send a message, that ain't just no manners! That's . . .
that's—"

He stopped, at a loss for a word to express behavior more
reprehensible than bad manners. Link noted that on Sord
Three "manners" had come to imply all that was admirable,
as in other places and other times words like "honour" and
"intellectual" and "piety" and "patriotic" had become syno-
nyms for "good." And, as in those other cases, something
was missing. But he said,

"Thana and I already tried duplying it, Harl. The duplied
one doesn't work, just as duplied knives don't hold an edge."

Harl stared at him.

"Sput! Y'sure?"

"Quite sure," said Link. "We solved the problem of the
knife, but the raw material to make a duplied stun gun is
rare everywhere. We haven't got it and I wouldn't know it
if I saw it."

Harl said "Sput!" again, and began to pace up and down.
After a minute and more he said bitterly;

"I'm not goin' to let my Household starve! So far's I know
no man has ever killed an ufft in a hundred years. They
act crazy, but they can't hold a spear to fight with, even if
they could make 'em. So it'd be a disgrace to use a spear on
them. But it'd be a disgrace to hang a man just because the
uffts wanted him hung! And to let 'em search our houses
any time they felt like it, just because they can't fight! Anyhow I'm not goin' to let my household go hungry because
uffts say they've got to!"

He stamped his feet. He ground his teeth. He started for the doorway. Link said,

"Hold it, Harl! I've got an idea. You don't want to use spears on uffts."

"I got to!"

"No. And if you use the only stun gun on the planet, it'll make them madder than ever."

"Can I help that?"

"You don't even want them to stop trading with your Household, greenstuff for beer."

"I want," said Harl savagely, "for things to be like they was in the old days, when the old folks were polite to the uffts and the uffts to them! When humans didn't need uffts and tools were good and knives were sharp."

"And everybody had beans for breakfast," Link finished for him. "But I've got an idea, Harl. Uffts like speeches."

Harl scowled at him.

"They like my speeches," added Link.

Harl's scowl did not diminish.

"I," said Link, "will go out and make a speech to them. If they won't listen, I'll high-tail it back. But if they do listen I'll gather them in a splendid public meeting with a program and orations about . . . oh, work hours and fringe benefits or something like that. I'll organize them into committees. Then I'll adjourn them to a more convenient place."

Harl said cagily,

"Then what?"

"They'll have adjourned away from any place near your Household, and you and your forty or fifty unicorns can go guesting and come back with your food. And," said Link, "meanwhile the uffts will be talking. And talking is thirsty work. That will be an urge toward negotiations by which the uffts can get themselves some beer."

Harl continued to frown, but not as deeply. After a time he said heavily,

"It might fix things for now. But things are bad, Link, an' they keep gettin' worse. This'd be only for right now."

"Ah!" said Link briskly. "Just what I was coming to! In your guesting, Harl, you will talk to your hosts about the good old days. You'll point out how superior they were to now. You'll propose an assembly of Householders to organize for the bringing back of the Good Old Days. That, all by itself, is a complete program for a political party of wide and popular appeal!"

"Mmmmmmh!" said Harl slowly. "It's about time somebody started that!"

"Just so," said Link. "So if Thana will fix me up a light lunch—the uffts had no food for Thistlethwaite to eat—I'll go out and try a little silver-tongued oratory. With all due modesty, I think I can sway a crowd. Of uffts."

Harl's frown was not wholly gone, yet. But he said, "I like that idea of goin' back to the good old days!"

"If you're allowed to define them," agreed Link. "But in the meantime we'll let the uffts talk themselves thirsty so they'll have to bring in greenstuff to get beer to lubricate more talk."

Harl said, very heavily indeed,

"We'll try it. You got words, Link. I'll get you a unicorn ready. That's a good idea about the good old days."

He disappeared. Thana said,

"You didn't finish telling me about Imogene."

"Oh, she must be married to somebody else by now," Link told her. "I'd wonder if she wasn't. Anyhow—"

"I'll fix you a lunch," said Thana. "I think you're going to accomplish a lot on Sord Three, Link!"

He looked startled.

"Why?"

"You," said Thana, "look at things in such a practical way!"

She vanished, in her turn. Link spread out his hands in a gesture there was nobody around to see. He heard a faint,

109

faint noise. He pricked up his ears. He went to an open door and listened. A shrill ululation came from somewhere beyond the village. It was the high-pitched voices of uffts. A rhythm established itself. The uffts were chanting,

"Death ... to ... men! Death to men! Death to men!"

VIII

AN HOUR LATER, Link went streaking away from the Household, urging his unicorn to the utmost, while Harl led shouts of anger and irritation among the houses. Another rider came after Link. His mount had been carefully selected, and it had no chance at all of overtaking Link. Then came two other riders, one shortly after another, and then a knot of nearly a dozen, as if pursuit of Link had begun as fast as men could get unicorns saddled for the chase. They rushed after Link with seeming fury. But he had a faster mount, a distinctly, pre-arrangedly faster animal.

But it was not the most comfortable of all animals to ride. Unicorns jolted. They put down their large and tender feet with lavish and ungainly motions, the object of which seemed to be to shake their riders' livers loose. The faster they traveled, the more lavish the leg-motions and the more violent the jarring of the man riding them. The drooping fleshy appendages which dangled from their foreheads flapped and bumped as they ran.

Link's pursuers seemed to strive desperately to overtake him. They shook fists and spears at him as he increased his lead. He topped a hillside half a mile from the Household, went down its farther slope, and squealed insults from uffts' throats seemed to give the Household posse pause. When Link was out of sight the voices of invisible uffts hurled epithets at his pursuers. The chase-party slackened speed and finally halted. They seemed to confer. Uffts shouted at them. "*Murderers!*" was a mild word. "*Assassins!*" was more frequent. "*Shame! Shame! Shame!*" was commonplace.

The men from the Household, as if reluctantly, turned their mounts homeward, and uffts came scuttling across the uneven ground to shout, "*Cowards!*" after them, and more elaborately, "*Scared to fight! Yah! Yah! Yah!*" As the riders pressed their mounts, the uffts became more daring. Rotund small animals almost caught up with the retreating spear-bearers, yapping at their unicorns' heels and shouting every insult an ufftish mind could conceive.

When the mounted men reentered the village, however, the uffts went racing and bounding to see what had happened to Link. The painted message on the *Glamorgan's* fin had represented him as pro-ufft, while Thistlethwaite was represented as having villainous intentions toward them. And Link had made them a noble speech, presenting a problem that could be arued about indefinitely. The important thing, though, was that he had fled from the Household, with pursuers hot on his trail. If the humans of the Household disliked him enough to chase him, uffts were practically ready to make him an honorary member of their race.

He kept up his headlong flight for a full mile. Then he gradually slackened speed, as repeated glances to the rear showed no sign of his pursuers. Presently he ceased altogether to urge the unicorn he rode, and proceeded at a leisurely, bumpy walk.

He became aware that uffts trotted or galloped on parallel courses to see what he would do. At first they did not show themselves, and he only caught fugitive glimpses of one or two at a time. But there were evidently some hundreds of

111

them, staying out of sight but keeping pace with him on either side.

He reined in and waited.

Uffts' voices murmured. There were even squabblings in low tones, as if uffts behind boulders and just behind hilltops were arguing with each other over who should go out into plain view and open a conversation. The buzzing voices became almost angry. Then Link let his unicorn move very slowly to one side while voices mumbled indignantly. *"Who's afraid of him?" "You are, that's who." "That's a lie! You're the scared one!" "... Then if you aren't scared, go out and talk to him!" "You do it! ... Huh! I dare you to go out and talk to him!" "But I double-dare you!" "I triple-dare you .... I quadruple-dare—"*

Then Link's head appeared above a hilltop, and the uffts knew that he could see a close-packed mass of them trying to insult each other into making the first contact with him.

"My friends!" said Link in a carrying voice. "I put myself in your hands! I ask political asylum from the Householders and tyrants who are your enemies no less than the enemies of every person in favor of your being favored!"

Every ufft gazed at him. Those nearest him tended to look scared. But Link waved his arms.

"On a previous occasion," he said splendidly, "I spoke to you of the galaxy-wide admiration of your intellect, and presented to you a problem the logicians and metaphysicians of other worlds have found unsolvable, though some solution must exist. At that time I did not realize that the sociological-economic conditions of your life had driven you to revolt. I was not aware that you were actually and unthinkably expected to earn the beer so necessary to the higher functions of the intellect. I did not know that you, the most brilliant race in the galaxy, were frustrated by a caste system of which you were less than the highest grade. But I began to suspect it last night, when you made a political demonstration in the Household streets. I confirmed it this morning. And when I expressed by indignation that uffts, here—uffts, my friends!—were not gladly supported by the humans who should listen to them with reverence, when I learned of the unbelievable withholding of the subservience due you—"

Link listened interestedly to himself. A man who doesn't believe too firmly in his own importance can often overhear remarkable things if he simply starts to talk and then leans back to listen. One's mouth, allowed to say what it pleases, sometimes astonishes its owner. Of course, it sometimes gets him into trouble, too.

Link found himself waving his arms splendidly while he passed from mere flattery to exhortation, and from exhortation to the outlining of a plan of action. He didn't like to disappoint anybody, and the uffts were capable of disappointment.

A part of his mind said wrily that he was making a fool of himself when all he needed was to get the uffts to move off so Harl could get away with a pack-train of unicorns and return with some unicorn-loads of groceries. But another part of his mind went on grandly, not disappointing the uffts.

"Your revolution," he told them eloquently, "has the sympathy of every lover of liberty, of license, and of uffts! I look to see the spontaneous uprising you have already made become the pattern for a planet-wide defiance! I look to see committees formed for correspondence with uffts on all this world! A committee to coordinate the publicity which will draw all uffts to your standards! I look to see committees for the organization of revolutionary units! Every talent possessed by uffts must be thrown into the struggle! Why not a committee of poets, to phrase in deathless words the aspirations of the ufftian race? My friends, I ask you! Who favors a committee of correspondence, to inform the whole planet of your intolerable grievances! Who favors it?"

113

There was some cheering. Nearby uffts cheered raggedly. Those farther away cheered because those nearer cheered. Those quite beyond the reach of Link's voice cheered because there was cheering going on. But those far-away ones were not following developments closely. A more-than-usually-fanatical ufft cried shrilly, "Death to all humans!"

"Splendid!" shouted Link valorously. "Now, who favors a committee to form revolutionary units for the liberation of the uffts?"

Those nearby cheered more loudly. Again, from the fringes of the gathering, there came bloodthirsty outcries.

"The ayes have it!" Link cried triumphantly. "Who's for a propaganda organization to stimulate the patriotism and the resolution of all uffts, everywhere?"

There were more cheers.

"Who volunteers for the Ufftian Revolutionary Council, to determine the policies which are to make uffts independent of all humans and raise them to their proper, inalienable position of superiority?"

Cheers. Yells. Uproar.

"My friends!" roared Link. "It is not befitting the glorious traditions of ufftdom that the Ufftian Provisional Government meet on the edge of a human Household, spied upon by humans! Let us march to some strictly ufftian area where the ufftian world-capital will presently appear! Let us plan this metropolis! Let us organize our revolt! Let us march forward, shouting the slogans of ufftian freedom! Who marches?"

There was an uproar of cheering which was distinctly heard and unfavorably reacted upon in the Household from which Link had seemingly fled a short time before.

With a grandiose gesture, Link set his unicorn in motion, headed in a distinctly general direction. There was a stirring, and presently innumerable plump animals, with pinkish skin showing through the sparse hairiness, came trotting and galloping to be close to him. He leaned in his saddle and addressed those nearest him on the right.

"Will someone volunteer to lead the cadence of the march?" he asked. "We should have marching units, chanting the principles of this splendid revolt. Leaders, please!"

Voices clamored to be appointed. He appointed them all, with definitely non-specific wavings of his hand. He gave them a march-cadence chant. They tried it as a group and almost instantly abandoned the group to lead other groupings. Link knew by intuition that anybody who wants to talk like the uffts, would want to lead others of his kind. It seemed that immediately there were half a dozen assemblages of uffts gathered about voluble, self-appointed leaders, giving out a rhythmic outcry,

"*Brackety-ax, co-ax, co-ax! Onward, onward, uffts! Brackety-ax, co-ax, co-ax! Onward, onward, uffts!*"

"That for the right wind of the Army of Liberation," he observed profoundly to those on his left. "Chant leaders? Who will lead the chants?"

Uffts by dozens vociferously demanded to be appointed. He appointed them all. He furnished them with slogans. Shortly there were bands of the pig-like creatures swarming over the countryside shrilling,

"*Uffts triumphant! Uffts supreme! Uffts are now a single team!*" There was another, "*Uffts have risen up to fight! Tremble, tremble at their might!*" A simpler one was still more successful, "*Uffts, uffts, on our way! Uffts, uffts, rise and slay!*"

The aboriginal population of Sord Three—the uffts—spread over an astonishing area as they scrambled up hillsides and flowed down the descending slopes. Those with satisfactory slogans to chant tended to stay more closely together, and to shout more loudly. Link's inventiveness gave out, and he appointed a Committee for Marching Recitatives to create other slogans and to pass on words of genius devised by anybody who happened to consider himself a genius.

There was much squabbling, and some remarkably blood-thirsty marching chants were devised, but the committee throve.

With a fine disregard for practicality but a completely sound estimate of the voluble mind, Link established all committees in an admirably vague state so any ufft who wanted to belong to any committee *ex officio* became a member. He tossed off committee titles with abandon. The Committee on Logistics for the Army of Liberation. The Joint Chiefs of Staff. The Strategy Council of the Ufftian Army. The Committee for Propaganda. The Committee on the Ufftian National Constitution. The Committee of Committeemen for the Coordination of the War Effort. . . .

There were hills in the distance, and Link more or less headed for them. The afternoon sun was hot. The ground was only thinly covered with vegetation. It was probably a good idea to head for an area where herbivorous creatures like the uffts could find something to eat. The hills looked green. And they might be cooler.

He set the marching pace at a comfortable strolling rate. He was leading the uffts who earlier had been besieging Harl's household and shouting insults at its inhabitants. He was creating the diversion needed for Harl to take a pack-train to a neighbor's Household and stock up with foodstuffs to endure a siege.

He found his role congenial. He liked novelty. He liked excitement. On occasion he enjoyed tumult. The present situation supplied all three. He was almost regretful that it wouldn't last. He considered it certain that when the Ufftian Army of Liberation got tired of walking, it would sit down on its haunches as quadrupeds do, and rest, and get discouraged, and eventually go home. Meanwhile, though, he was a generalissimo of a strictly improvised army.

There were troops of uffts scrambling up hillsides and down again, shrilling, "*Brackety-ax, co-ax, co-ax! Uffts! Uffts!*

Uffts!" The original marching-slogan had been modified. Link admitted to himself that it was improved. His Committee for Marching Recitatives had, astonishingly, turned out some others. As time passed they began to appear spontaneously in ever-forming and ever-re-forming groups of uffts. They continued to appear in new forms as the afternoon wore on. There were other signs of initiative. Uffts came galloping to his side to identify themselves as—self-appointed—commanders of the rear-guard, the scouts, the Undefeatable Reserves, the Ufftian Commandos, the Rangers, the Guerillas and other military groups, and to tell him that all went well with their commands. They went away with their appointments confirmed by his acceptance of their reports. In some cases they simply went off to form the units they had just designed for themselves.

Sunset approached. The hills grew higher and steeper. The vegetation grew less sparse. Link began to be astonished by the persistence of the uffts in what he'd thought would be not much more than an hour or so of dramatic make-believe. He began, indeed, to worry a little.

There were deep shadows on the hillsides when an ufft from the self-appointed advance-guards came galloping back from the leading part of the march. He pranced splendidly in a half-circle, came alongside Link's unicorn, and said in a strictly military manner,

"General, sir, the colonel in command of the advance-guard asks if you wish to occupy the abandoned human Household in the valley to the left, sir. He suggests that for logistic reasons it may be a suitable temporary headquarters. There's a large spring, sir, with good water. What are your orders?"

"By all means occupy it," said Link. "We'll at least bivouac there for the night."

But he blinked at the now-steep hillsides around him. It was almost dark. The situation began to seem less than merely amusing. The uffts really meant this revolt business! He hadn't taken them seriously. It was not easy to do so now. They acted like children, to be sure. But children would have gotten tired of this play-acting and marching long ago. Children, indeed, would have abandoned the encirclement of Harl's Household.

It occurred to Link that the uffts had more brains than he'd credited them with. They were desperately concerned about the stun gun with which they'd been peppered the night before. If such weapons were to be available to the humans on Sord Three, the uffts would be in a very bad fix. They couldn't fight back. They had little hoofs instead of hands, and their brains were of no use to them because they lacked fingers and especially an opposable thumb.

Naturally, in the presence of human co-inhabitants of Sord Three, they had to lie to themselves to be able to endure their handicap. They pretended to despise humans. They were childishly bitter. They scornfully said that to have hands instead of hoofs was a shameful thing. But they knew, just the same, that the introduction of stun guns on Sord Three would make them utterly helpless as against humans. So with a naive desperation they were taking the only action they could imagine, under the only leadership they could consider qualified. It was not wise action. It could hardly be effective action. But Link felt obscurely ashamed of himself. He'd started it.

The hillsides to right and left became steeper and the valley in which the Army marched became deeper. Link saw his following more or less as a mass for the first time. There were some thousands of the uffts. They would have covered an acre or more in the closest possible marching order. Spread out, they were an impressive lot of creatures.

Here there was a band of a hundred or more, keeping close together and silent for the time being. There was a knot of twenty or thereabouts, chanting a slogan as they

118

marched. He noticed that they looked weary. They also looked absurd. And they were totally unsophisticated in such practical matters as self-defense against men mounted on unicorns and carrying spears. They could be hunted down as corresponding creatures have been hunted down on ten thousand colonized worlds. The only difference between them and the wild lower animals of other planets was the uffts had brains. But brains in the absence of an opposable thumb left them ridiculous.

The swarming, now leg-weary small horde of uffts swung into a narrower valley which entered this one from the left. Far up this second valley there were human structures. Even in the gathering dusk they could be seen to be abandoned. The valley walls were almost precipitous. Rock strata of varying colors alternated in slanting streaks of stone. Link saw a stratum of extremely familiar peach-colored stone. He shrugged his shoulders.

The uffts flowed on, in small clumps and big ones, some few as individuals, many in pairs. Weariness was breaking down the undisciplined bunching of the march. They were now merely a very large number of very weary small animals, sturdily following Link's leadership because he'd made a speech, and they couldn't do much but make speeches themselves, and so could not estimate the uselessness of speechmaking.

Some of them began to hurry, now. There was a small stream, which dwindled to a thread down the valley up which Link now rode morosely. Near the deserted and crumbling structures it was larger. At its source it was a considerable spring. Link saw crowds of the uffts drinking thirstily, and moving away, and being replaced by others.

His own escort—he realized suddenly that some uffts had appointed themselves his personal escort and staff—moved on to the human structures. The roofs of the smaller buildings had collapsed. The household or village must

119

have been abandoned for many years. The largest structure would correspond with Harl's residence. It had been the residence of the Householder of this place. Doors had fallen. Windows gaped.

Link's escort stopped before it.

"I suppose," said Link, "that I'd better take this over as my headquarters."

"Yes, sir," said an ufft's voice. "You'll give us more orders in the morning, sir? You've plans for the War of Liberation, sir?"

"I'll make them," said Link. He was vexed.

He dismounted, and many small aches and pains reminded him that a unicorn is not the most comfortable of riding animals. He went into the abandoned Householder's residence to survey it while some little light remained.

Inside was desolation. There was furniture remaining, but some of it had collapsed, and some was ready to fall of its own weight at any instant. There was a great hall, with an imposing chair of state like the one in Harl's great room. The flooring of the great hall was stone. Link gathered bits of dry-rotted furniture and kicked them. They fell apart. He built a fire, as much to cheer himself as for warmth.

Thana had prepared a lunch for him. He hadn't had time to consume it. It was bread and beans, but there were three plastic bottles of beer. Link ate a part of the bread-and-beans lunch. He started to drink one of the bottles of beer.

Then he looked up at the chair of state upon its dais. He shrugged, and again started to open the beer. But again he stopped.

With the flickering fire for light, he went over to the chair of state. He searched, and found a button. He pressed it. There were creaking, groaning sounds. The chair of state rose toward the ceiling. Something excessively dusty rose out of the pit beneath it. It was a duplier. Link stared at it.

120

THE DUPLICATORS

"It won't work," he told himself firmly. "It can't! They abandoned this place because it stopped working!"

It would have been sufficient reason. If the art of alloying steel had been lost, and even the art of weaving, and if agriculture had been practically abandoned, certainly nobody would have remembered how a duplier worked, to repair it when it broke down.

But Link tried the device. He put a scrap of wood in the middle bin, for a sample, and another scrap of wood in the raw materials bin, and pressed the button. The duplier sank into the pit and the chair-of-state, creaking, descended to the floor. The button again. The process reversed. The duplier came back into view.

It hadn't worked. Nothing had happened.

Link went back to his tiny fire. He brooded. He liked novelty and excitement and sometimes tumult. He had none of these things about him now. He scowled at the firelight.

Presently he took a burning brand and went back to the duplier. He looked it over. It was complex. It utilized principles that he could not even guess. But there were wires threading here and there. He blew away the dust and stared at them.

One had rusted through. At another place a contact was badly rusted. Insulation was gone from a wire, which thereby must be shorted. He shifted the wires to find out how many were broken or whose contacts were loose.

He was irritated with himself, but the reasoning was sound. If nobody remembered even vaguely how electrical apparatus worked—and Harl said that there used to be lectric but it existed no longer—and if nobody bothered to understand, maybe they didn't know what a short-circuit would do! They might not even understand what a loose contact could do!

He used up four torches, fumbling with obvious defects which any ten-year-old boy on another planet would have observed. Eventually he went back to the button. He pressed it. The duplier and after it the chair of state descended. He pressed the button once more and they rose in their established sequence.

The duplier worked. A scrap of wood in the materials hopper had almost disappeared. Another scrap of wood—a duplicate of the one in the sample bin—had appeared.

Link went out and barked orders. Uffts came tiredly in the darkness. Link took off the embroidered shirt he wore.

"I want some greenstuff," he said firmly, "and I want this shirt soaked in water and brought back dripping wet."

He hunted for more furniture to build up his fire while his orders were obeyed. Presently he put his dripping shirt—uffts could hardly carry water in any other manner—with branches and weeds into the duplier. He put one of his three bottles of beer in the sample hopper. He pressed the button.

Shortly he owned four bottles of beer. The plastic containers were made out of the cellulose of the greenstuff stems. The beer was made out of the organic compounds involved and the water brought in the saturated shirt.

There was, then, a very, very great stirring in the darkness about the abandoned household. Uffts excitedly foraged for greenstuff about the buildings. Weeds grew high. There were trees. Some were small, but some were of considerable size because this human Household was abandoned. Link necessarily duplied his shirt so that more water could be brought by uffts who had no other way to carry it. The chair of state ascended and descended and rose and sank down again.

When Link lay down to sleep on a very hard floor, it was late at night. The morale of the Ufftian Army of Liberation was high. Excessively high. He'd taught some uffts how to keep the duplier in operation with thirty-two bottles of beer in the sample hopper. The duplier worked steadily.

THE DUPLICATORS

Outside, in the darkness, uffts chanted gloriously, in splendid confidence of all the future:

> *"General Link, what do you think?*
> *Brought his army here!*
> *When he stopped, up he popped*
> *Passing out bottles of beer!"*

Link went to sleep with various uncoordinated choruses chanting it. But he wasn't easy in his mind.

In fact, he had nightmares.

IX

LINK MADE a speech next morning. He'd hammered out, very painfully, the only possible action he could advise or command his followers to take. Essentially, it was to take no action at all. But he couldn't put it that way. It was obvious that if the culture of the human inhabitants of Sord Three had deteriorated because of the lack of contact with the galactic civilization, the status of the uffts had diminished, too. But it was also absolutely certain that if there had been contact with the rest of the galaxy, there'd have been hell to pay.

At the least, every duplier on Sord Three would have been taken forcibly away by adventurers landing with modern weapons and no scruples whatever. As a side line, such space-rovers would have come upon the uffts. They'd have kidnapped them and sold them as intelligent freaks on a thousand worlds while one planet after another collapsed into chaos as a result of the dupliers. Ultimately, in fact, the citizens of Sord Three would have starved for the lack of dupliers while the rest of the galaxy went hungry because it possessed them. Transported and enslaved uffts would have been involved in the collapse of human civilization, and the galaxy at large would have gone to hell in a handbasket.

It was still a strong probability. Link was the only person anywhere who realized it. If it was to be prevented, he had to do the preventing. The responsibility was overwhelming.

Therefore he made his speech.

"My friends!" he said resoundingly, from an extremely rickety balcony in the outer wall of the householder's crumbling residence. "My friends, it is necessary to decide upon a policy of action for the realization of the objectives of the Ufftian Revolution. Let me say that when I came here to ask your help in the solution of an abstract question, I did not realize the emergency that existed here. I urge that the problem, my problem, of the barber and who shaves him be put aside for the duration of the emergency. All the resources of the ufftian race, including its unbelievable intellect, should be devoted to the single purpose—freedom!"

There were cheers. They were more prompt and louder than the day before, because Link had appointed a Committee for Emphasizing the Unanimity of Ufftian Opinion, and they cheered whenever he paused in the course of an oration.

"You are here as an army," said Link, oratorically, "and an army you should remain. But you are the most intelligent race in the galaxy. Therefore it is natural for you to adopt the most intelligent strategy for the achievement of your ends. Your master strategists have undoubtedly discussed that classic of military doctrine, *Power in Space* and have determined to apply the principle of the space fleet in being to the basic problem of this war, so ensuring ufftian victory."

THE DUPLICATORS

He paused, and cheers rose confusedly in the morning sunlight.

"An army in being," announced Link profoundly, "is an undefeated army. By the fact that it is in being, it has proved that it is undefeatable. To be an army in being is to be a victorious army, because if it were not victorious it could not continue to be! Therefore the first item of Ufftian policy is to keep the army in being and therefore to keep it undefeated and victorious, an inspiration of uffts everywhere, drawing them to join it and share in its glory and its triumph!"

Cheers. The Committee for Emphasizing the Unanimity of Ufftian Opinion took its cue more promptly, and there was a high, shrill tumult of approval, much greater than before.

"Specifically," said Link with a fine precision, "the policy of the Ufftian Provisional Government is to maintain its army in being, to spread propaganda everywhere to cause uffts everywhere to join and increase that army, to cause its enemies to realize the futility of conflict, and ultimately to make a generous and equitable peace which shall realize all Ufftian national aspirations and establish the Ufftian Nation in permanent, unquestioned, and unquestionable solidity!"

Cheers now echoed and reechoed from the walls of the valley. Link held up his hand for attention.

"In pursuance of this policy," he said valiantly, "we shall immediately organize the Committee for Propaganda upon a new scale. We shall enlarge the organization of G-1 and G-2, our intelligence and counter-intelligence groups. More volunteers for this necessary work are needed. We shall need volunteers to explain the policies of the Ufftian National Constitution to the uffts who will shortly join the Ufftian Revolutionary Army. We must have volunteers for security services, for communications, for espionage, for education, and for a survey of the cultural monuments and purposes to be preserved and obeyed, and for the preparation of a history—a detailed history—of this epoch-making and unanimous uprising of all uffts for the realization of these traditional aims! And—"

It was an admirable speech. When he'd finished, his hearers were almost hoarse from their cheering. He retired into the tumble-down householder's residence with a forlorn kind of satisfaction. He was still the leader of the revolution. The uffts believed they were going to accomplish something unique under his guidance. It was conceivable that they might. No ufft could possibly topple him from his post as leader, because all uffts knew that they were inexorably restricted in achievement by the fact that their hands were hoofs. They could only believe in accomplishment associated with hands. There could be uffts wrought up to sabotage or crime by a purely ufftian leader, but Link alone could be the nucleus around which a genuinely large number of uffts would gather.

There were two main reasons for it. One was his psychological advantage in that he could make speeches and had hands besides. The other was discretion. He'd asked for volunteers for innumerable committees and high-sounding boards and councils. But he hadn't even referred to the organization of combat units. The Ufftian Revolutionary Army was prepared for propaganda, espionage, education, counter-espionage, and probably social services and psychoanalysis. But Link had at no time suggested that anybody get ready to fight.

An important but subsidiary reason was the free beer issued by the Quartermaster Corps to any ufft or group of uffts who came into the great hall of state, dragging a reasonable amount of greenstuff and a sufficient number of water-soaked shirts, ready-duplied for the transport of water required in beer. Unquestionably, the free beer helped.

Its appeal showed up on the second day of the revolution-

ary movement. A little knot of traveling uffts, some twenty
in number, were halted by security uffts as they crossed the
mountains on private business of their own. They were
questioned, given beer, and turned loose. Half of them did
not leave. The rest went on to tell their friends and bring
them back. Various of the original marchers appointed themselves recruiting officers of glamorously named organiza-
tions and went home after new members. They got them.

By the third day there was a steady trickle of volunteers
for the army and especially the civil service of the provisional government. They came through mountain passes
or across the rolling foothills toward the formerly human
household. By the fourth day, the loss of ufft-power was
noticeable in human households as much as fifty miles in
every direction. Harl's household reposed in a vast tranquility.
Groups of pack-animals could go and come between neigh-
boring households without even a shouted *"Murderers!"*
flung at them along the way. But all the householders were
faced with the need to go guesting to get needed foodstuffs.
There were no more ufft-carts coming in with greenstuff.
There was no general strike, of course, but the result was
the same. Uffts were gathering at the Ufft Future World-
Capital up a rather steep small valley, where anybody
could have all the beer he wanted for the greenstuff required to make it. Link had started out with perhaps two
or three thousand followers. Four days later there were
twenty thousand about the former human settlement. Some
of the uffts, females, no doubt, disapproved of the bivouac
idea. Permanent burrows began to appear here and there.

From time to time Link performed some ritual to remind
the uffts that they were a revolutionary army. On one occasion he presided over a marching-recitative competition,
when small bands of uffts marched past his residence chanting vainglorious doggerel for inspirational purposes. The
slogans, of course, stressed loyalty to the principles of the

Provisional Government, the National Constitution, the Declaration of Freedom, the Appeal to Intellects, and so on.

On another occasion he solemnly led an organization down the valley to where a vein of very familiar peach-colored rock showed in the valley wall. He picked up a fist-sized bit of it, fallen out of the vein, and carried it back to the Household. He placed it as the first stone in a six-foot-high cairn of peach-colored rocks to mark the place where the Ufftian National Bill of Rights would presently be adopted. It hadn't been drawn up yet. Discussion of its details required much beer, and the self-appointed committee to compose it had to spend so much time hauling the necessary greenstuff that not much time was left for deliberation. It was already apparent to Link that in the absence of ufft-carts, the beer dragged to the duplier cost more time and effort per bottle than when it could be hauled on wheels and humans took a toll of it.

But matters in households nearby had become serious. There were practically no uffts remaining as hangers-on about human villages in a very large area. A space roughly two hundred miles across was denuded of uffts. It extended from the sea to the eastward of Link's headquarters, well beyond the mountains in which he commanded. In some of those households, men had actually been forced to gather greenstuff or go hungry. The fact caused anti-ufft feeling to run high. Already it had occurred to Link that if he could find another abandoned household with a duplier as readily repairable as this first one, he could start a new center of ufftian independence. Given dupliers and shirts or their equivalents to carry water in, uffts could have beer at will, or almost so. They gained no other tangible benefit from their association with humans.

Paradoxically, it was Link's own doing that counter-measures against the Revolution began. When Harl had spoken so bitterly in favor of the good old days, Link had agreed

128

with him. He'd suggested that Harl call an assembly to bring about their return. It was a suggestion with infinite appeal. Everybody can think of good old days they'd like to recall. No two people will want to recall the same good old days, but the theory is attractive.

Harl fumed at the desertion of the uffts who had made his household a liveable place. He argued the matter with other householders forlornly traveling about trying to get food without working for it. They tended to agree more furiously as the number of uffts on their households dimminished, and the conditions more nearly approached the real good old days when Sord Three was first colonized.

Link continued depressedly to be the acting head of the Ufftian Provisional Government, the Ufftian Army of Liberation, the Coordinator of the War Effort, and a considerable number of other things. He drank a bottle of beer occasionally. For other subsistance he had to depend on duplied repetitions of the lunch Thana had made for him. It was a fair lunch, but it was a horribly monotonous diet. But there was nothing he could do about it. He was followed everywhere by devoted uffts who—it was irritatingly touching—seemed honestly to believe that they were getting somewhere.

Perhaps they were. At any rate, by the fact of their absence they impressed the humans with the necessity for their presence. They made endless speeches to each other. They drank innumerable bottles of beer. And they stripped the valley of greenstuff. At the end of a week they were dragging branches two miles to get beer. In nine days the production and consumption of beer began to fall off. The work required was more than even beer was worth.

Link envisioned a change in the food-provision policies of human households on Sord Three. Given agricultural machines, and seed of modern breeding, one not-too-skilled man could plough, cultivate and make ready for harvesting an enormous acreage. Uffts could weed it. Uffts could harvest it. They could enter into a real symbiotic relationship with humanity. And he was beginning to think of a way to secure the alloy materials and rare-element supplies needed for the restoration of lectric and vision-casts, synthetic fibres and fabrics, and probably means of transportation superior to unicorns. He grew wistful as he pictured it to himself. Sord Three could become a paradise, and dupliers could be used for a new purpose so effectively that their original function would become forgotten. The economic system of Sord Three could gently be diverted to something really intelligent.

Link felt himself qualified to design an intelligent economic system. He'd have liked to talk to somebody about it. But the only suitable listener on Sord Three would be Thana. Making his plans, he imagined himself explaining them to her.

When disaster came, Link was absorbed in the design of a flexible new economic order which would eventually be able to stand visitors without disturbance, and the visitors would not be disturbed by what they found. Dupliers would not be recognizable as such, and so would be harmless. Designing such a system was an appalling problem, but Link attacked it valiantly—until disaster arrived.

A party of uffts brought a newcomer to the tumbledown building Link inhabited alone. The newcomer was abusive and rebellious.

"Sir," said a Security ufft in a stern voice, "here's a spy, sir. He came from Old Man Addison's Household. He was sent to spy out our military secrets."

"Yah!" snarled the spy. "You haven't got any military secrets! There's dozens of us, and we know all about everything you do! We're a tight organization and Old Man Addison knows every secret of every household and every ufft town, and if you hurt me he'll know who did it and get even!"

He glared defiantly about him.

THE DUPLICATORS

"He'll know, eh?" said Link. "Maybe somebody's already telling him about your capture, eh?"

"That's right!" snapped the spy. "You don't dare hurt me!"

Link reflected. This was in a way a court martial, except that Link was the only judge. The great hall with its chair of state was dusty and littered. The plump and angry uffts who'd brought in the prisoner made indignant noises.

"Now," said Link pleasantly, "you have a chance to be a double-spy, a very high rank in your profession. You begin by telling us everything you know about what the Householders are planning in this war."

The spy-ufft made raucous noises of derision. So Link said sternly,

"We'll assemble the army. It will march past where you're held fast. Every member of the army will take one nip at you. Just one. Nobody will kill you, but somewhere in the process of receiving some tens of thousands of nips—"

The spy squealed. Link had expected it. There were not less than forty thousand uffts either in the Army of Liberation or the committees associated with it. The total might be as high as fifty thousand. The spy instantly agreed, shaking with terror, to tell everything, everything, everything.

"Take him away and question him," said Link in an official voice.

An hour later he received the report. The spy had told everything. On demand, he'd identified other spies. They'd been questioned separately, under the same threat. Their stories checked. So far as the revolt was concerned, the disaster was absolute.

Harl had begun the organization of Householders for the Restoration of the Good Old Days. There was great, grim approval and much disparity in the definitions of the good old days, but there was unanimity about present days. An ufftian army of liberation in being, equipped with a Household with a working duplier and able to supply beer with no benefit to humans, that could not be endured! House-holders had mobilized their retainers. They were armed with spears. Some four or five hundred humans were gathered at Old Man Addison's household. On the morrow they would march on the Provisional Capital of the Ufftian Provisional Government. They were prepared to kill uffts with spears. They would.

That report to Link had not been completed when the Committee for Counter-Espionage clamored for his ear. Their operatives had reported substantially the same appalling facts. Members of G-1 and G-2 came galloping. The news had been brought to them. There was agitation. There was tumult. There was terror.

"My friends," said Link in stately sadness, "the cause for which we were prepared to suffer and die has had a set-back. The immediate success of the Revolution is now questionable, but its final success is certain! It would not be intelligent for uffts, who are the most intelligent beings in this galaxy, to throw away their lives with anything less than certainty of its sheer necessity. But this is not true of this moment. There is action by which the Revolution can continue. There is work to be done—organization, propaganda, planning! We shall . . . we shall go underground!"

It was the most lucid and most convincing of all pos-sible phrases. Uffts lived in burrows. Underground. They pre-ferred them. They meant safety, uffishness, the familiar, the normal, and the most satisfying way of life. Underground? Uffts cheered . Spontaneously!

"From this time on until the next occasion for rising," said Link splendidly, "the Provisional Government will exist in secret. The Army of Liberation will exist in the hearts of its members! And all uffts, everywhere, will remember that time marches on, life is short but war is long, in union there is strength, and the uffts will rise again! The Army will scatter. Its members will hold close the secrets of its association. And presently—"

He waved them out. Naturally, though privately, he was very much relieved. He knew that Harl, certainly, would not dream of trying to single out individual uffts for punishment for their part in the revolt. For one thing, it would be impossible. For another if he did the uffts would run away again. The other Households would have the same imperative reason for ignoring so far as possible the revolt of the uffts. It was even likely that they'd take some pains to keep from having much discontent among the uffts who at their own will could move from Household to Household or settle where they were best satisfied.

There was one matter in which Link was less than satisfied. He wasn't sure that householders like Harl would be moved to reestablish agriculture to the point where food could be had without dupliers. It was necessary for the far-away plans Link already debated. But he wasn't sure it was going to happen. Yet.

But he had one personal reason for overwhelming relief that he could resign as generalissimo of the revolt. He'd been living on duplied rations, replicas of the lunch Thana had prepared for him days ago. In the nine days since, that lunch had gotten deplorably stale. But it was worse than that. In nine days of the same eatables, Link had gotten almost hysterically sick of beans.

He watched a ceremonial march-past of the Army of Liberation before it dissolved into individuals and family groups headed for their home burrows and a vociferous denial that they'd been in the Army at all.

But he'd reserved one unit of some two hundred uffts, privately asked to volunteer for a last item of military service against their oppressors, in case they should be needed. They were members of the Ufftian Diehard Regiment. They listened sternly and even devotedly when he gave them their instructions. They seemed to disperse like the rest. But—

When they were gone, he was alone in the decaying Household. There was something that needed to be done, and only he could do it. He worked nearly all night by very indifferent torchlight. When dawn came he cleared away the evidence of his labor. He brought up the duplier from its pit for the last time. Painstakingly, he re-shorted a formerly shorted wire. Wires that had been broken he re-separated. Loose contacts he turned into no contacts at all. The duplier would duply no more.

And in the early morning he rode to meet the army of householders and their retainers. In a sense, of course, he was going to surrender. But he felt sure that his explanation would satisfy Harl and therefore the rest. But as he rode, his mind was not on such matters. It dwelt hungrily upon pictures of food that would not be beans.

He met the approaching army a dozen miles from his former headquarters. He was mistaken about his explanation satisfying the householders, however. Harl was visibly distressed both by his explanation and its reception. Thana, riding with Harl—she was the only girl with the armed expedition—looked at Link inscrutibly.

The human army halted to pass upon Link's behavior. Thistlethwaite glowered at Link and loudly disclaimed any association with him at all. He was no longer Thistlethwaite's junior partner. He was—

They made camp, to discuss the situation in detail. Then Thistlethwaite was astonished to be placed in the dock as Link's fellow-criminal. The head of this court martial would be Old Man Addison. He was not an amiable character, and Link took an instant dislike to him. His air was authoritative and offensive. His speech was very far from cordial. Link found that his objection to Old Man Addison could be summed up in the statement that he didn't have any manners.

But he knew what he intended the court martial to do,

and he plainly meant to see that it did it. Against Thistle-thwaite's arguments he said acidly,

"You stuck me once. I gave you a spaceboat cargo on your promise to come back an' pay me adequate for some dup-liers. You're back. Where's the stuff you was to bring?"

Thistlethwaite protested despairingly.

"You' goin' to be hung," said Old Man Addison, as acidly as before. "An' I take your ship to pay me for what you cheated me out of. And any more strangers land on Sord Three get hung right off, no questions an' no foolin' around!"

The court martial convened. Link explained lucidly that the uffts around Harl's household were already nearly in revolt, that they'd besieged Harl's Household, and that with Harl's approval he'd gone out to persuade them to go off some-where and let pack-trains of unicorns relieve the food shortage. He pointed out that he had accomplished exactly that. He even pointed out that no human had been insulted or injured by uffts following his oratorical suggestions. He'd assumed leadership of the uffts as a favor to Harl.

Harl cast the only vote in the court martial in favor of Link. The decision was that Link and Thistlethwaite were to be hanged the next morning. The delay was to allow other householders, hurrying to the scene, to watch the pleasant spectacle.

Link remained composed. Especially after the number of uffts usually to be seen about a gathering of humans ap-peared, one by one, and moved casually about the en-campment. Nobody bothered them. It was the habit of hu-mans to tolerate uffts. By midday there were at least fifty uffts moving about among the men and tents and animals. Later there were more.

Near sundown, Thana was admitted to the closely guarded place where Link and Thistlethwaite waited for morning and their doom. Thana looked at once indignant and subdued.

"I'm . . . sorry, Link," she said unhappily, "Harl's still

arguing, trying to get them to change their minds. But it doesn't look like he's going to! He's even told them that you showed me how to duply a knife so it's as good as an unduplied one! He's promised to make them all presents of shirts and beans and unduplied knives! But they listen to Old Man Addison."

"Yes," admitted Link. "He has a certain force of character. But his manners—" He shook his head. "Even Thistlethwaite doesn't approve of Old Man Addison now!"

Thana caught her breath as if trying not to cry.

"I . . . I brought you a shirt, Link. I . . . guess you didn't like that embroidered one. You took it off. This is duplied from the one you gave Harl."

"Hm," said Link. "Fine! Thanks, Thana."

She wept. He patted her shoulder.

"Is there anything . . ." she whispered, "is there anything I can do? Anything, Link!" She sobbed. "I . . . feel like its my fault, you being in trouble. If I'd had more food stored away you wouldn't have had to lead the uffts away and . . . and—"

Link said helpfully,"

"If you feel that way, why . . . a couple of unicorns up the valley at midnight— If you could manage that, I'd appreciate it a lot!"

She was silent. Then she said bitterly,

"You . . . you want to go back to Imogene!"

Link stared at her.

"Look, Thana, I didn't tell you the end of the story! After I got on the spaceship, and that's nearly a year ago, I looked at the receipt the florist had given me. And he'd written down Imogene's address on the back of the receipt. So he couldn't send the flowers or the note. So Imogene never heard from me again, and if I know her she's married long ago!"

She looked at him earnestly.

136

"Honestly, Link?"

"Of course," Link said with dignity. "Have you ever known me to lie?"

"Where shall I have the unicorns?" she asked. "And how?"

"Influence," said Link. "I've got influence. Now—"

He told her a place it would not be easy to miss, perhaps a mile up the valley from the camp. She went away.

He seemed absorbed in thought for a long time after that. He didn't even pay particular attention to the uffts which near sunset seemed to increase in number. But once an ufft winked reassuringly at him. Thistlethwaite was bitter, but Link consoled him as well as he could.

"You," he said kindly, "mistake the courtesies of business life for sentiments of deeper importance. You should reform."

Thistlethwaite swore despairingly at him.

Darkness fell. Stars shone. The camp quieted. Then, at midnight, there was sudden and dithering uproar. Tents collapsed. Unicorns made dismal noises, tried to bolt, and finding their tethers bitten through by uffts, high-tailed it for the mountain slopes, with heel-nips to urge them on. Men swore, under blanketing canvas. Men tried to run after the unicorns and uffts ran between their legs and upset them. Those who tried to haul collapsed tents off their fellows suffered similarly irritating upsets. When swearing men crawled out to the open air, uffts nipped their legs and they leaped madly. There was a swarm of shouting uffts all about, ripping at any human or other heel within reach, biting through any ropes that remained intact, and bellowing contradictory orders in fairly good imitations of human voices. They turned the camp into something close to primordial chaos.

Link grunted as one of his own guards was bowled over. He grabbed at Thistlethwaite. He led the way. A small party of uffts formed around them, clearing the path. Twice, householders or their retainers seemed about to blunder into them, but each time they toppled as running uffts hit their knees from behind. Then the entire escort ran zestfully over them in what they considered the fine tradition of the Diehard Regiment. Before disbanding his army, Link had picked them out, dramatically, for possible secret military action. This was it.

He and Thistlethwaite arrived where the unicorns should be. Around them, their escort boasted of their achievement in releasing Link. He had to warn them that these unicorns, dimly seen in the starlight, were not to be stampeded.

Then he discovered that there were three unicorns, not two. Thana flung reins to Link.

"Come on!" she said fiercely. "Maybe they'll follow!"

"I've got a rear guard," said Link, tranquilly, "and you'd better not come with us, Thana. Better turn your unicorn loose and get back to the camp."

"I won't!" said Thana. "I told Harl what I was going to do. He asked me to apologize for not coming to see us off."

"Us?" Link's mouth dropped open. Then he felt good. Remarkably good. He said warmly, "Harl has the best manners of anybody I know!"

They headed up the pass down which Link had come to surrender. The unicorns climbed. Thistlethwaite fumed and sputtered. He'd built a most extensive structure of dreams upon a supposedly firm business engagement with Old Man Addison. It was now wrecked. And Old Man Addison considered that he should be hanged. *And* the gait of riding-unicorns was excessively unpleasant. But he followed, dismally, the resolute figure of Thana, silhouetted against the stars. Link's figure was often close to it. Very close.

In an hour they were over the pass. Thana would have led the way on past the narrow valley in which the Provisional Government had functioned for nine days. But Link turned the animals into the valley-bottom and took the others up to the Ufftian Provisional National Capital.

THE DUPLICATORS

"There's something in the former Householder's home that I want to pick up," said Link. "I worked all night at it."

By the time they reached the dreary building, Link had solved the fastening of the saddlebags before him on the unicorn. They were quite large enough for his purpose. He dismounted and pointed out where a cairn of peach-colored rocks had been considerably reduced in size. He explained to Thana why it had been partly pulled down, and what he wanted to carry away. When they entered the great hall of the chair of state she was with him. He showed her what he'd used the peach-colored rocks to be raw material for.

"Pretty!" said Thana.

She helped him with his burden. They had to make two trips, filling up the saddlebags. They remounted and headed down the valley again. Thana said interestedly,

"They're beautiful! I never saw anything like that before!"

They went on. And on. And on. When the hills were well behind, Link said,

"Thistlethwaite, you welded up everything, including the lifeboat blister. Where's the oxygen torch?"

Thistlethwaite sputtered a reply.

"We can't use the ship," said Link cheerfully. "With at least one hull-plate torn off and general structural weakness all over, we'll have to use the lifeboat."

Thistlethwaite mumbled. A faint, faint light glowed, far away.

"That's the Household," said Link. "Harl's Household."

"Y-yes," said Thana in a singularly small voice.

"We can take you there."

"Do you want to?"

"No!" said Link explosively. "No!"

The feeble light in the Household was a guide. Presently they came to the ufft city and the unicorns' night-vision helped them avoid both the burrows and the mounds of dirt dug out from them. They heard querilous, frightened voices around them. Link stopped.

"My friends," he said profoundly, "this is Link Denham, escaped from your oppressors. I go to function as a government in exile and to prepare for the resurgence of the Ufftian race! I will be back with the means to resume the struggle of the uffts to attain that recognition, that status, that independence of humanity which is their justified aspiration!"

There were cheers, but they were only half-hearted.

"Meanwhile," boomed Link, "follow us. In the ship there are gifts and treasures. You might call them the treasury of the Ufftian Republic. We will distribute them. You may use them in bargains with men! Follow us!"

To Thistlethwaite he said cheerfully,

"I'll pay for the cargo."

Thistlethwaite said bitterly,

"If I can't get it away, I don't want Old Man Addison to have it!"

They went across the city. They were accompanied, escorted, surrounded by a swarm of uffts. They went beyond the city to the ship. Thistlethwaite swearing corrosively, produced the oxygen torch.

There came squealings from the distance. Men on unicorns were headed for the ship. They would be, of course, pursuers of Link and Thistlethwaite, who hadn't spent any time in a diversion like a trip to the Ufftian National Capital. Link reassumed command. He ordered the uffts to bite the heels of the riding-unicorns, to try to disperse and in any case to delay their pursuers. With a fine, brisk competence he took the oxygen torch and cleared the lifeboat blister so it could be entered and the lifeboat used. He heaved the saddlebags into the boat. He began to open the cargo compartments for the uffts. They swarmed into the ship. As a compartment door came open, they rushed in. They would be rich. They

could make beautifully insulting bargains with the humans of
Sord Three. They could—

There was faint, faint gray light to the east. Link cut
his way into the control room to get the *Galactic Directory*.
He came back.

"Where's Thana? Where's Thana?" He grew alarmed.

She appeared, scared but smiling.

"I . . . wanted to be sure you'd . . . miss me."

He bundled her into the spaceboat with the directory. He
shoved Thistlethwaite in after her. He opened the outer
doors of the lifeboat blister and shouted to the swarming
uffts below.

"I shall return! I shall return!"

There was a knot of riding-animals coming from the west.
Uffts scurried and raced about them. The men on the unicorns advanced only very slowly in consequence.

Link leaped into the spaceboat. He pressed appropriate but-
tons and moved appropriate levers. The lifeboat seemed to
topple outward. Its rockets roared furiously, it surged ahead.

It was a near thing. Lifeboats are designed to be launched
in space. But the nose of this one swung skyward, and its
rockets thrust steadily and violently upward, and presently
their roaring changed in that subtle fashion indicating
pure emptiness outside the spaceboat. Then it leaped toward the star-filled firmament.

Days later Thistlethwaite worked zestfully, with a porten-
tious scowling, upon a new contract he proposed to Link. It
was to form a new organization, the Sord Three Development
Corporation. Link was to provide the entire working capital.
Thistlethwaite was to have the final say in all business decisions. The details of the operation had been thrashed out

in conversation, and Thistlethwaite was putting them into business phraseology, with at least one booby-trap in each two paragraphs of the contract. Link would purchase and lead up a first-class modern spaceship. He would carry back to Sord Three samples of all needed alloying materials. He would establish a duplier by the seashore to remove from flowing sea water—as raw material—the rare minerals needed to duply the large inventory of new, currently undupliable objects and instruments needed on Sord. Link, privately, had designed beer-making equipment intended to be run by uffts. There would be enormous dislocations of the present economy when uffts didn't need to trade with humans for beer. Humans would start to grow vegetation. They would, in fact, start to grow crops. Their dupliers would be more valuable extracting alloying metals than duplying roots, barks, herbs, berries, blossoms and flowers.

There would be hell to pay on Sord Three when Link went back. It would provide novel experiences. Exciting ones. From time to time there would doubtless be tumult. But if no other ship landed on Sord Three for just a very few years, when another ship landed there'd be no disaster. There'd be no dupliers in action. Nobody would recognize the galaxy-wide disaster that could be brought about if certain mineral-extracting devices, working on sea-water, were put to other uses. Everything would be swell!

Link pointed out a small crescent against the stars to be seen from the lifeboat's ports.

"We're going to land there?" asked Thana.

Link nodded. Thana said in a low tone,

"Link, are you going to sign that contract he's drawing up?"

"Of course not!" said Link. "But it makes him happy to write it. Actually, he'll like the deal I'll give him better than the trick one he's contriving."

Thana said uneasily,

THE DUPLICATORS

"When we land—"

"I'll go to see a jeweller," said Link mildly. "I'll sell him a few carynths, a quart or so. I'll start things working for our return trip. And then— Do you mind a quiet wedding?"

"N-not at all."

He nodded. They held hands as the lifeboat headed for the planet before them. There were seas, and continents, and ice-caps. There were cities. Four saddlebags full of carynths would hardly all be sold on one planet without breaking the price, but a discreet distribution by spaceship to responsible jewelers in other worlds—

"We can start back," Link promised, "in a month or so."

And they did. But they were delayed a few days, at that. Link had arranged for something special and they had to wait for Thana's second carynth necklace to be finished. It was said that she was the only woman in the galaxy who owned more than one.

www.ingramcontent.com/pod-product-compliance
Lightning Source LLC
Chambersburg PA
CBHW050758250626
47155CB00005B/2118